RUBICON ESCAPE

SUPERNATURAL APOCALYPTIC WAR

BOOK 1

TODD OCKERT

Cover design by Fins and Feathers Designs
Editing by Helen Thornton-Gussy, Edit Co.

First published 2024
Second edition published October 2025 by TALA Media LLC

Paperback ISBN: 978-1-968643-07-2
Hardback ISBN: 978-1-968643-08-9
eBook ISBN: 978-1-968643-06-5

Acknowledgement

I want to extend my heartfelt thanks to my wife for her steadfast support and belief in me, which made this book possible. This is my first attempt at writing a work like this. Her deep interest in herbs and teas inspired me to include them, and I plan to explore these subjects further in future editions of this series. I also find inspiration from reading literature in this genre.

I am grateful to Del Albright for reviewing this manuscript and offering constructive feedback. He introduced me to the Rubicon Trail and the Friends of the Rubicon (FOTR), enlightening me on the organization's mission and history. Together, we worked as Trail Bosses during volunteer weekends with FOTR, committing our time to preserving the trail for future generations to enjoy.

Chapter 1

The Trail Shifted

TJ

I turned to John. "You feel that?"

He stopped beside his Jeep, his expression darkening. "Yeah. It's like the air's charged," he said as he rubbed his arms. It was cool at this altitude, though not cold enough to give us a chill.

I grabbed the handheld radio clipped to my vest and pressed the mic. Nothing. No crackle, no feedback. Just dead silence. The screen had no display to indicate what channel or frequency I was on. I pulled out my phone—black screen. It wouldn't turn on, even with a hard reset.

"My radio's dead," I said, my voice low. "Phone too. No signal, no power. Like they've been fried."

John frowned and pulled his own phone from his pocket. He held the power button down and waited. Nothing.

"You thinking what I'm thinking?" I asked.

He nodded slowly. "EMP."

My gut clenched. The realization landed like a punch to the ribs.

"Shit," I muttered. "If it were a nuke, we may or may not have seen the flash. The other option is that it could have been a CME or Coronal Mass Ejection from the sun that killed everything. I doubt it, though, as we would have seen the northern lights last night with one that big."

John scanned the tree line, his head swiveling side to side, looking for something. His hands were resting on the butt of his pistol.

"I agree with you on the two options for killing our electronics. How widespread do you think it is?"

"Either one would kill everything, though, if it's what I think it is, everything with a circuit board just died. Planes. Cars. Power grid. Internet. Satellites." I swallowed. "Everything."

I looked at John and noticed his eyebrows knit together, one creeping higher than the other, rubbing his jaw, and staring like his question was stuck in the back of his brain. I'm sure I was giving him the same look as my forehead creased, and my mouth hung open like my brain was stuck in neutral.

"We need to get off this trail—now," I said. "Get to the ranch, check on the wives, secure everything."

John gave a curt nod. "Let's move. You find Todd, I'll pack."

I jogged toward the caretaker's cabin, Ruffus trotting at my side, his ears perked up, and nose twitching like he smelled danger. "Todd!" I called out, my voice echoing off the granite walls. No answer. The place was empty.

"Where'd he go, boy?" Ruffus tilted his head and nudged my leg, eyes wary. He didn't bark—just stayed close, as if he felt it too.

I looked back down the trail toward camp, every instinct screaming at me to hurry. Something had changed in the world. We just didn't know what that something was, or how bad it might be.

When I returned, John was standing next to his loaded Jeep, arms crossed, scanning the ridgeline. Even his usual sarcasm was gone.

"Hurry up, Swabbie," he said—but there was no bite to it this time.

I forced a grin. "You could've helped pack."

"You could've moved faster," he shot back, but he didn't even smirk.

As I packed, the silence deepened. No aircraft overhead. No distant engines. Just the whisper of wind across the granite slabs and the occasional creak of the pines. Even Ruffus, usually excited to hit the trail, stayed close to my side, tail low, his eyes watching the horizon like he expected something to come crawling over it.

And maybe he was right.

Both our Jeeps were older CJ models with no onboard computers, which meant they were EMP-proof and ready to roll. We each towed small trailers with rooftop tents, with room enough for our wives when they joined us.

I thought about Mel and Shelly back at the ranch. I had no doubt they'd be fine—but if the EMP was real, and they were in town when it hit, they'd be stranded. Mel's truck was new and vulnerable. I just hoped they hadn't left yet.

"Hey John," I said as I secured the last strap, "I'm keeping my rifle and pistol ready—just in case. I know we're still in the communist state of California, or Commifornia as we commonly called it, but you never know what we might run into on our way home."

John grinned. "You know me. I'm always ready."

I watched John check his weapons over, his Smith & Wesson 9mm and an AR with a Vortex LPVO. I'd seen him hit steel at over 300 yards with that setup. "You going to mount your AR in your gun rack, or lay it across the seat and center console for the trip home?"

"I'm going to mount it in the gun rack, that way it doesn't slide around in the Jeep. I won't lock the rack, so I can get to my rifle quickly if it's needed."

"Copy." I placed my rifle in the rack and secured it without locking it fully into place. It would take me about two seconds to pull the rifle from the rack if needed.

"You worried about us being in this communist state?" John asked and then snickered.

"Not really. We have trained enough law enforcement personnel around here that they know us and would give us a pass."

"You ready for the trip out of here?"

"We were born ready. Let's get moving up the trail to home," I said as I placed the last items in the Jeep. "Ruffus. Load up."

Ruffus hopped into the passenger seat, gave me his best doggie smile as I climbed in.

Chapter 2

Dead Jeeps and Cold Truths

I focused on the trail as the Jeep bounced up the trail toward Cadillac Hill and Observation Point. This trail wasn't a scenic drive to the store, so I had to stay focused on where I placed my tire and Jeep. The cliff on the right side made me concentrate that much more. The small boulders and loose rock littered the terrain, forcing me into a slow crawl. It felt like every jolt and bounce was more amplified than usual. Maybe it was the silence, or the tension that was knotting my gut.

As I came around the corner of the trail, I saw two newer Jeeps with their hoods up, sitting in the middle of the trail, blocking our way. Four people—two men and two women — stood around them, clearly in the midst of an argument. From a distance, I could already hear raised voices.

John and I stopped, climbed out of our Jeeps, and approached cautiously, watching as the situation simmered just shy of boiling over. I could see the men were angry, red-faced, and shouting over each other, while the women stood back, arms crossed, visibly fed up. It didn't take much to figure out what was going on. The Jeeps were dead, stranded in the middle of the trail, and frustration was spilling over.

"Looks like they're not going anywhere," John muttered beside me, his hand resting near his hip.

I stepped forward. "Hey, I doubt we can fix whatever's going on with your rigs, but we can help move them off the trail so we can get through."

The taller of the two men turned to face me. He wore a faded John Deere hat with a tattered bill, a blue Pabst Blue Ribbon T-shirt, and baggy black shorts. His eyes narrowed. "You can just wait. We'll have 'em running in a few minutes."

"I don't think so," I replied, keeping my voice level. "Do you know what an EMP or a coronal mass ejection is? We think that's what hit us. All our radios and phones are dead. Yours probably are, too."

The PBR guy stared at me blankly. "Nope. Coronal what? No idea what those are."

"Let me explain it to you then. An EMP is a high-altitude nuclear explosion, and the resulting electromagnetic wave from the explosion kills all electronics, like your phone, the computers in your Jeep, and power grids. The other option is a coronal mass ejection (CME), which originates from the sun. The electromagnetic waves from it do the same thing as the EMP to the electronics," I explained.

When I looked at them, they both had blank stares. Finally, the PBR guy blinked twice, his gaze drifting somewhere over my shoulder. "Wait … what?"

"True as the gospel, dude."

PBR finally spoke again, his voice laced with skepticism. "I still think it's just a fuse or some crap. And if that's true, then why the hell are *your* Jeeps still running?"

I thumbed back to our Jeeps. "Ours are older, no computers, no chips. Yours probably fried the moment the pulse hit. We can use our winches to pull you out of the way. There's a flat spot about thirty feet up, perfect for you to work or wait."

While I tried to reason with PBR, I saw John drift over to the women. With our winches and straps, we could drag the Jeeps clear if the guys let us help. "We could even give you a ride off the trail. We're heading out anyway."

PBR folded his arms. "Not happening. I'll have them fixed in a jiffy."

I stepped back, giving them some space as I took a deep breath, then another.

The two women walked over to me, kicking rocks out of the way. "Great. This is going nowhere," she muttered through gritted teeth.

"I know. We can wait a little bit and try to reason with them again," I said, a little more relaxed, crossing my arms as I stood back, watching them play with wires and fuses under the hood.

"I'm Claire, and this is Tracy," the blonde one said. "Those dipshits are our boyfriends … at least until we get off this damn trail."

Both women were slightly shorter than I and were dressed practically. Claire wore a pink T-shirt with an AR-15 graphic and the words *Life of the Pew Pew*. Tracy had a brown ponytail and a black Nine Line shirt that read *Stop 22 a Day*. Both wore black 5.11 tactical pants. I could tell they were clearly not your average weekend campers.

I walked back to PBR. "Any luck?"

He didn't even look at me. "Still dead, obviously," he said with a growl to his voice.

Claire and Tracy muttered something under their breath. PBR turned to them. "What'd you say?!"

"You're being a pain in the ass," Claire fired back. "Let these guys move the Jeep. They even offered to take us into town so we can get parts—or whatever we need."

His hands curled into fists. "Just shut up. What do you know? You're just a girl."

He raised his hand to strike her.

He never got the chance.

John was faster. I watched as he drew his pistol, his movements swift, aiming center-mass at PBR.

"You hit her," John growled, "and today becomes the worst day of your life. You'll be catching lead before your hand comes down."

Ruffus released a low, menacing growl. He stepped forward, his teeth bared, and his eyes locked on the man.

PBR froze. His arm dropped. His eyes flicked from the pistol to Ruffus, then back to John. The fire in his posture extinguished quickly; his shoulders slumped in defeat, and he unclenched his fists

His buddy, Bob, if I remembered right, finally spoke. "Let's just move the damn Jeeps."

"Fine," he said through pinched lips.

"Ladies," I said, turning to Claire and Tracy, "would you like a ride off the trail? We can drop you at the trailhead or take you into Lake Tahoe."

Tracy let out a long breath, rolling her shoulders to relax them. "That would be great."

Claire nodded. "We live in South Lake Tahoe. If you could just get us into town, we can walk home from there."

"Done," I said. "Let's clear the road first."

John and I pulled our recovery gear from the Jeeps—tree straps, snatch blocks, soft shackles, the works. This section of the trail had enough anchor points, and with the winch cables, tree straps, and snatch blocks connected to their Jeep, we slowly winched them off the path. It took nearly an hour—slow, heavy pulling uphill—but our Warn winches and Factor 55 gear held up. When we finished, we loaded our gear and helped the women pack theirs.

Claire rode with me, Tracy with John. Ruffus gave up his seat reluctantly but accepted the bribe of extra ear scratches. He rewarded me with a wet snort against my ear before curling into the back.

As we bounced our way down the trail, we talked. I told her about my Navy career, the tours overseas, and how I'd built my life as a tactical shooter and trainer.

"Tracy and I are trauma nurses at the hospital in town," Claire said. "We've worked there for about three years. We met Jay and Bob at a bar. They seemed decent, so we went on a few dates. They invited us to go camping. We brought our own tent."

I shook my head. "You don't have to explain yourself to me. You're adults. And don't worry, I'm not hitting on you. I love my wife and have no reason to screw that up."

"I wasn't worried about that. They seemed nice enough," she said and smiled in a show of relief.

"If you're curious," I added, "I can explain what I think happened this morning."

"I'd appreciate that," Claire said.

"I believe a high-altitude nuclear detonation caused an EMP. Basically, everything with a circuit is fried. Phones, computers, cars, aircraft. It's all down. We're vulnerable now—and if someone wanted to invade, this would be the time."

"Why do you think that?" she asked, tilting her head, one eyebrow arching as if the words didn't quite line up in her mind.

"I have read a lot of stories about EMPs. Everything, from government white papers to fictional stories, mentions things like what we are seeing now. It makes us defenseless, and an opponent can use that to their advantage and attack."

Claire's smile faded. "Do you think the power in town will be out?"

"I'd bet on it," I said. "And in a few days, people will panic. Stores will run out of food, water, and medicines. Looting will start. Police will abandon their posts to protect their own families. Gangs will take control."

She turned to me. "I don't know what we'll do if it gets that bad. What are you and John planning?"

"I have a ranch near Minden. We're preppers. We have gardens, a greenhouse, livestock, and a secure bunkhouse for others. We're ready."

Claire turned back to look out the window. "What about the hospital? Medications, supplies … won't they restock?"

"Doubtful. Most new delivery trucks won't run. When hospitals run out, that's it. No resupply, no transports. If the hospital doesn't have security, it could get raided for the hard drugs."

"And the people?" she asked.

"Those at the hospital. Unless they have family or someone stays, they will most likely die a painful death of starvation and dehydration. The others in town. Most only have a few days of food. Once that's gone and the fridge goes warm, desperation will set in. If they have a generator and fuel, they'll make it last a bit longer. But most don't."

We crested Cadillac Hill, and I was relieved to pass Morris Rock and Observation Point without issue. The trail beyond was easier—about ten more miles to the main road. Two hours later, we reached the trailhead and stopped to air up the tires.

"Why inflate the tires now?" Claire asked.

"We air down for traction on the rocks. Makes the ride smoother, too. But on pavement, soft tires aren't ideal." I went back to concentrating on the tires.

Ruffus barked. I glanced over to see Tracy throwing a stick for him. I needed to have a word with that dog about flirting.

"We've got about fifty miles to the ranch," I said. "We'll pass through South Lake Tahoe and drop you off on the way. Town might still be quiet, for now. But that won't last. Most folks still think everything will turn back on like magic."

Chapter 3

Shelter or Risk

I stood up from airing up my tires, then grabbed some water out of the Jeep. I offered some power bars to Claire and Tracy to chew on before heading out.

"Ladies. We'll be in town shortly," I said. "I'd feel better dropping you off at your house rather than having you walk through town. Early in a disaster like this, things are usually calm—but that won't last."

"I agree," John added. "I hope you have weapons at home. Things are going to go sideways fast once people realize nothing's coming back online."

"I like the idea of you dropping us off," Tracy said, nodding her head slightly. "Our house isn't far off the main road. You'll pass it on your way through town. And yes—we both have weapons. We try to hit the range when we're off work from the hospital."

"Good," I said. "Let's get rolling, we're burning daylight."

We turned onto Highway 89 and headed into South Lake Tahoe. The drive was smooth until we reached the outskirts of town. We swerved around dead vehicles and avoided groups of people flagging us down for help. I saw some pointing at our Jeeps, their eyes wide. They were probably wondering why ours were still running when everything else had gone silent.

As we rolled through town, there were more abandoned cars. More desperate people. Ruffus barked or growled every time someone got too close, and that alone kept most of them back.

Claire pointed out the turn to their place, and a few blocks later, she motioned toward a small yellow ranch house with white trim, a well-kept lawn, and a detached garage.

I pulled to a stop in the driveway. "Nice place."

"Thanks," Claire replied. "It was my grandparents. They left it to me after they passed. It's paid off and solid. I appreciate the ride—and everything you two did to get us away from Jay and Bob."

I saw John and Tracy chatting as she climbed out of his Jeep. Ruffus let out a soft whine as Claire stepped out, his eyes following her and Tracy up the walk.

I turned to John. "Hey, you think we should invite them to the ranch? They've got solid skills, and we're going to need people like that to survive."

"I agree," John replied. "They'd be great assets. And we've got the space."

I stepped out and called after the women. "Claire! Tracy! One more thing—don't worry, it's not what you're thinking," I said, seeing their curious expressions. "We've got plenty of room at the ranch. You both have skills that could make a real difference. No pressure. You're free to leave anytime—but you'd be welcome."

Ruffus took the opportunity to stretch his legs and explore the yard. I saw his head swiveling as he tried to watch the women and the street.

Tracy hesitated. "Do you really think we'd be in danger staying here?"

"I'd bet on it," I said. "Towns like this have an ugly side. Once word spreads that law enforcement can't respond, the scumbags will crawl out of the woodwork. They'll come for food, meds, and women. Women will become a commodity, traded for drugs and protection.

If you've got weapons, you might hold them off, but not forever."

Claire exchanged a look with Tracy. "Give us a few minutes to talk."

They disappeared into the house, and I turned to John. "Think they'll bug out and come with us?"

"I do," he said. "Tracy and I talked about it on the way here. I laid out what they might face if they stayed here. Did you notice the crowds at the police station and the line outside the grocery store?"

"Missed that," I admitted. I looked back at the house as I heard the front door swing open. The women stepped out, determination in their stride. Their faces were set, eyes focused ahead as they moved purposefully toward our waiting vehicles. It was clear they had made a decision, and the doubts that lingered moments before seemed to have faded. United in purpose, Claire and Tracy walked side by side, ready to face whatever lay ahead with us at the ranch.

Chapter 4

Dogs, Guns, and Gut Checks

"We talked it over," Claire said. "If you'll have us, we'd like to come with you."

"We'd love to have you," I said. "Our wives will be glad for more company at the ranch. Grab your gear—clothes, weapons, anything important. Once we leave, it may not be here if you come back."

"We have a couple of suitcases, but we'll need more than that," Tracy said. "How should we pack?"

"If you've got totes, use those. If not, trash bags work in a pinch. You'll have rooms in the bunkhouse."

John headed inside with the ladies to help them pack.

I was standing at the Jeeps, thinking of heading inside to help, when Ruffus let out a sharp bark. I looked down the sidewalk. Two teens had turned the corner and were heading toward us. They wore worn-out jeans, white T-shirts with the sleeves cut off, red bandanas tied around their heads, and sneakers that had seen better days.

"Heel," I commanded.

Ruffus was instantly at my side, sitting tall and alert.

The boys stopped twenty feet away. The taller one smirked. "Hey, Pops. What're you doing with those fine chicks? You look a little old to be hanging out with girls like that. Might have to take them off your hands."

He spat on the sidewalk and puffed out his chest. "Heard the popo's got no wheels or radios now. Guess no one's gonna stop us from taking what we want."

Ruffus shifted his weight and let out a low growl, barely restrained. I turned slightly, keeping my pistol side away from them. Ruffus sensed my shift and leaned forward, the tension in his body like a coiled spring.

"You boys might want to keep walking," I warned. "Those women are more than you can handle—and so's my dog. You stick around, you'll be his new chew toy."

"You're funny, old man," the tall one said. "Juan here could kick your ass with one hand tied behind his back."

The shorter one grinned and flipped open a folding knife.

I drew my pistol.

"Whoa, old man—we's just kidding," the short one stammered, trying to fold the blade back into his pocket.

I motioned with my pistol. "Turn around and keep walking, or I'll put you down like a rabid dog."

They hesitated, then turned and started walking away mumbling something incoherent.

"You might want to run," I added, "because I might change my mind."

Ruffus let out a sharp, angry bark, followed by a menacing growl, his teeth bared. I watched them bolt, almost tripping over themselves in their hurry to get away.

John returned with an armful of packed bags and started loading them into the trailer.

"Hey, slacker," he called out, "there's more inside."

"Someone had to protect the Jeeps from the local scumbags," I shot back.

"Sure, Swabbie," he muttered.

Claire and Tracy came out with two bags each, both wearing pistols on their hips.

"Nice work strapping up," I said. "You just missed two punks who had their eye on you. I ran them off."

Her lips parted slightly, her breath caught as she seemed to struggle with how quickly civilization was descending into chaos. "Already?" she asked.

"Word's spreading that the cops are grounded and silent. It's only going to get worse," I warned. "How much more do you have?"

"Just a few small items—and our rifles and ammo."

"Alright. We'll finish securing the gear out here. Be ready to roll."

They came out with their remaining gear a few minutes later and locked up the house.

"Hey John," I said as I pulled a map out and laid it on the hood of my Jeep. "Let's continue through town and catch Stateline. From there, we will take Highway 50 over to the 207, and that will allow us to work southeast to Highway 88, and home."

"Sounds like a plan, and I think it is the best route from here," he said.

My stomach tightened. The route sounded straightforward, but my gut instinct was telling me otherwise.

"Load up," I called to Ruffus. He jumped in and took his usual spot in the passenger seat. I tapped him on the head and pointed to the back seat. He gave a huff but obeyed.

Claire climbed in and began stowing her AR-15. "There are two options for securing your rifle. The rack is one place, though; you can also put the barrel down on the floor and hold onto the stock. If you need to get out quickly, you can pull the stock to your shoulder easily," I said.

"Thanks, and that makes sense."

"You might want to load a magazine or two," I said. "Just in case."

"Good idea," she replied. "Do you expect trouble on the way to your ranch?"

"I don't expect it," I said, "but I plan for it. Better to be ready than caught scrambling."

She nodded. "Smart."

As we drove through town, I asked, "What do you know about weapons? What pistol are you carrying?"

"My AR's a basic build from a local shop," she replied. "My pistol is a Sig Sauer P320 AXG. Tracy and I train a couple of times a year. Our dream is to attend a Ghost Ring Tactical course in New Mexico. Those guys are top tier."

"They run a great program at Ghost Ring Tactical, though you'll get plenty of training at the ranch," I said. "We've got a range and drills ready to go. I'm a competitive shooter—so we train with movement, not just punching paper."

Claire smiled. "I got the P320 from my dad when he passed last year. I've had my eye on the P365 XL Rose with the Romeo Zero Elite. Feels better in my hand, though the 320 holds more."

I smiled. "My wife, Mel, carries the Rose edition. She loves it. From now on, I think we'll carry twenty-four seven—except when we're sleeping."

Claire chuckled, but I caught the same tension in her eyes that twisted in my own chest. She glanced over, quiet for a moment.

"Do you ever feel like we've crossed a line, TJ? She asked, voice softer than usual.

I nodded, keeping my eyes on the road ahead. "Yeah. We left normal behind a while ago."

She looked out the window, then back at me. "You think we'll ever get it back?"

I shook my head, resolute. "No. There's no going back now."

She sighed, but her grip on the pistol tightened. "Guess we'll just have to keep moving forward."

"That's all we can do," I replied.

Chapter 5

The Bridge Ambush

The road was running smoothly under the tires after turning onto Highway 207. Scanning the area around me, I saw a roadblock a little way in front, stretching across a bridge. I tapped my brakes, giving John notice that there was trouble ahead. He was a few hundred yards back, and I knew he'd proceed with caution after seeing my brake lights light up.

The roadblock came into full view as we finished rounding the bend. I hit the brakes hard and rolled slowly forward to assess the situation. Several vehicles were angled across the road to block our lane, with debris and other junk scattered around.

"If I were setting up an ambush," I muttered, "I'd block the far side of the bridge to trap folks in the middle. Amateurs who don't know better."

"This might get dicey," I added, my voice low. "Be ready for anything."

"Copy," Claire replied, her voice tight.

A heavyset man emerged from behind one of the vehicles. He waddled out confidently, smiling at us as he raised a hand to stop us. He was enormous—at least 300 pounds with a mouthful of rotting teeth and a stained white T-shirt stretched tight over his gut. His jeans looked painted on, and the frayed legs dragged over worn-out sneakers. He clutched a chipped, mismatched AR-15, the paint flaking off in brownish layers.

I stopped about ten feet away. Ruffus growled from the back

seat, and from my side mirror, I could see him push his head out of the window, his ears flat and eyes fixed on the fat man in front of us.

"What do I do?" Claire asked.

I scanned the rearview mirror. "Follow my lead." I couldn't see John. I hoped that meant he had pulled off and was setting up his overwatch.

I watched Fat Boy swagger closer. A couple of heads popped up behind the vehicles, which I assumed were his backup. "Roll your ass up here!" he called out, his words slurred and smug. "We've got questions before you go any further."

Ruffus barked sharply, pushing further through the window. I cracked my door and stepped out, positioning myself so Ruffus had a clear path if needed.

"What do you want?" I asked, already scowling.

Fat Boy's beady eyes darted to Claire in the passenger seat. "I want the lady and your ride," he said, grinning. "Figure I'd show her a good time."

"You're not getting either," I growled, my hand tightening on my pistol.

The barrel of his rifle came up, aimed square at my chest.

A bloody third eye appeared on his forehead. The round continued through his skull, and removing the back half, brain matter and blood splattered the pavement behind him. He wobbled on his feet for a moment before collapsing backward in a wet, lifeless heap.

I drew my pistol and raised it, scanning for movement behind the cars from Fatboy's friends that I had seen a little bit ago. Their eyes were wide open, jumping between me and the dead form on the ground. Stepping forward, I kicked the AR away from Fat Boy, even though I knew he was dead. Claire jumped out of the Jeep, her pistol in hand, and shouted toward the blockade. "Hands up! Show yourselves!"

Multiple voices came from behind the vehicles. "Don't shoot! Don't shoot!"

"Step out where we can see you!" I yelled. "If you're armed, we will shoot!"

Ruffus leapt from the Jeep and barked again, snarling as he stalked forward.

Four men emerged, hands in the air, clearly terrified.

"We're not armed!" one of them said. "Our weapons don't work—George and his crew took the firing pins."

I studied the man who had spoken. Tall and lean, with close-cropped hair, he wore a polo shirt with a logo I didn't recognize and expensive-looking jeans. He looked completely out of place.

"Who are you?" I asked.

His words came out quickly. "My name's Billy. That guy you just killed—his name was George. He and a few others forced us to stand guard with disabled weapons. Mine's just a prop now."

"You're telling me George was in charge of this blockade?" I asked.

Billy glanced at the corpse. "Yeah, I was heading to the store to get food for my family when this all started. They kidnapped them, told me to stand out here to intimidate travelers. They didn't care that the weapons didn't work. Said fear was enough."

"You know what happened?" I asked.

Billy nodded, his eyebrows pulling into a frown. "EMP. I'm shocked they figured out so fast that law enforcement couldn't respond."

I saw John approach the body, looking over his shot.

"Clean." I heard him say quietly. He bent down to pick the AR up and inspect it. Then in a louder voice, he asked, "So what now?"

"We move the vehicles, rescue Billy's family, and get back on the road."

"Rescue?" he echoed with a groan.

Billy stepped forward, a look of fear on his face. "Please. My wife and kids are at a camp just up the road. These thugs aren't that many, but they're violent."

I turned back to the others. "What about you?"

One of them raised a hand. "We live nearby. We'll walk home."

"Fine," I said. "Take nothing. Move off the road and keep your heads down."

John's eyebrows raised, he tilted his head slightly to one side, and he smiled. "Let's go save a family," he said, checking his rifle.

Like we would just leave them here, I wondered if he was thinking that. "Agreed, but this time, let's be the ones setting the trap."

Chapter 6

The Cost of Collapse

"We're burning daylight—let's move," I said, moving to the dead vehicles.

I put my shoulder into the back fender of the dead vehicle, and with a grunt, started pushing, creating a path for our Jeeps.

Billy climbed into the back seat with Ruffus. Claire jumped into the passenger seat beside me. Ruffus gave a sharp chuff right into my ear, making his opinion known about sharing his space. I gave him a quick scratch. "Sorry, buddy, we'll be home soon."

Thinking about how quickly this all spiraled rattled me. I'd read plenty of books from authors who predicted that chaos would erupt within three to five days after an EMP or grid failure—but this was only the beginning, and we were already running into roadblocks, armed gangs, and hostage situations.

Billy, though, struck me as someone useful—trained, adaptable. The kind of man we needed at the ranch.

"Billy," I said, glancing back at him in the rear-view mirror. "You and your family are welcome at our ranch. We don't have space in the Jeeps for all your personal items, but if you're willing to join us, we'd be glad to have you. What does your wife do?"

"After today?" he said, his voice tight. "I know she'll want to leave. Joanne's a teacher and a master gardener—she's got a degree in horticulture. She was home today for an in-service." He went quiet for a moment. "Oh, and the gang has a truck that still runs—they've been using it to move people."

"Sounds like we can take their truck once we free everyone," I said. "John and I have trained for situations like this at the ranch and our range. We'll get your family back."

Billy leaned forward and pointed over my shoulder to a dirt road on the right. "Turn down there."

I turned in, leaving enough space for John to pull in behind me. "How far?" I asked.

"Just over half a mile," he replied. "There's a small clearing ahead where we can park."

The Jeep rattled underneath me as I drove down the dirt road. I eased into the clearing and backed the Jeep in, nose facing the exit. John did the same. If things went south, we could pull out fast.

"Alright, team. Gather up," I said. "Billy, we need eyes on their setup. Can you draw us a basic map of their setup?"

"I can," Billy said, and knelt to draw a crude map in the dirt. "I've seen eight guys total. Most carry bolt-action rifles. Two have ARs, but they're in bad shape. I overheard them discussing the need to guard three bridges, which suggests there might be five left at the camp. They've got families locked in the buildings on the left."

"John?" I asked. "Plan?"

"As much as I'd like to have Claire and Tracy with us, someone's got to stay with the Jeeps," he replied. "We don't know if they have another crew out kidnapping. Our mobility matters. Leave Ruffus to guard them—he won't let anything through."

Ruffus wasn't pleased about staying behind, but I pointed to Claire and Tracy and told him, "Protect." He sat and locked onto them. I trusted him with my life—and theirs.

John led us through the trees. We moved fast, using the cover to mask our approach. Smoke drifted from a burn barrel at the center of the camp. Around it, four men were grilling steaks and vegetables—smells that made my mouth water despite the tension.

"Left house—is that the one with your family?" I whispered to Billy.

He nodded.

I couldn't see the others, so we pulled back. "Any access from the rear?" I asked.

"Maybe," Billy whispered, "the windows have bars."

Did they install those, or were they there prior to the EMP?"

"I don't think they just installed them. This area is kind of rough, and a lot of houses have bars on their windows around here."

John and I circled around, checking. Steel bars. Getting in that way would make too much noise. "We'll have to breach from the front," I said to John, my voice low, "and that means a firefight."

Two more men stepped out from a house and joined the group at the fire.

"Six confirmed," John said quietly. "We spread wide—same drill as back at the range. I'll take the two on the right, you and Billy split the rest."

I moved behind a tree on the left, Billy was behind a large rock, and John was using another large tree as cover. As we got into position, I looked at John to watch for the count to begin our attack.

John started the countdown using his left hand and fingers. On "one," he grabbed the guard and squeezed the trigger.

His suppressed rifle popped twice in quick succession. The first bullet entered one man's temple, spraying brain matter across the guy next to him. Before the second could even process what had happened, he took a round through the nose.

Billy froze. I swept left, double-tapping the first threat in the chest. Blood sprayed as the man crumpled. My second target turned, but my round hit him in the sternum. A follow-up shot took out his neck.

John spotted Billy's indecision and covered him. Another clean shot dropped one more. I picked off the last, my round punching through his heart and sending him into the dirt.

Billy breathed heavily, his rifle shaking.

"Sorry—I couldn't line up the shot," he stammered, breathing heavily, sweat dripping from his forehead. "Never had to shoot anyone before."

"It happens to just about everyone the first time they have to shoot someone. If you get used to it, then I might start to question your sanity," John said, looking at me. "You okay?"

"I'm good," I replied. "Might catch up to me later."

We watched the shack door for movement. Nothing.

John and I moved in, going from room to room, and we cleared the building quickly. No hostiles. We headed for the building where Billy's family was being held. I kicked in the door, yelling, "Friendlies! Hands where I can see 'em!"

We cleared the rooms fast—no enemies. Just wide eyes and tied wrists.

We secured the house and brought the families outside to reunite them. Billy dropped to his knees and hugged Joanne and the kids. I gave them space—it was a moment he needed.

John and I pulled him aside afterward.

"I know this is all happening fast," I said, "but we believe the power's out across the country—an EMP. That's why everything's dead. Our ranch is near Gardnerville. We're set up, self-sufficient. You're welcome there. Rules are simple—pull your weight, and don't be an ass. Sorry—language. We've got room for all of you."

"I appreciate that," Billy said. "Let me talk to Joanne."

Billy turned and walked away to talk to his wife. John and I went to check the gang's old red Dodge Power Wagon.

John bent down to look at the chassis. "Paint's shot, but the tires looked decent. It'll do."

Billy and his wife returned a few minutes later.

She looked up at me, studying my face. "My name's Joanne. This is Melissa, she's fifteen," Joanne said, pointing, "and Charlie, he's twelve. We'd like to come with you."

"Glad to have you," I replied. "Let's roll out. We'll stop at your place so you can pack what you need."

We drove back to the clearing where Claire and Tracy were posted up behind the Jeeps.

"Don't shoot—it's us!" I called out.

Ruffus bolted toward me, tail wagging. He licked my hand a couple of times, then sat at my feet, vibrating with excitement.

"Billy," I said, "we'll follow you to your house. Grab food, clothes, whatever you can carry. Trash bags work fine. Kids, bring your favorite game or toy. Joanne, any quilts or heirlooms—don't leave them."

I looked at their two-story eggshell-blue house with a red front door and a wrap-around porch. It appeared peaceful. Ordinary.

"Thank you for taking us in," Joanne said. "I've got some family quilts I can't leave behind."

"You're welcome. I've read enough post-apocalyptic fiction to know that survival depends on building a community or a MAG. Strength in numbers."

"What is a MAG?" Joanne asked.

"That is a Mutual Assistance Group, or a group of people who come together to share resources and help each other survive disasters."

Outside, I saw Charlie playing with Ruffus. The two of them chased each other through the grass, laughing and barking.

I lifted the final load into the truck's cargo bed and turned to Billy. "Stay about two hundred yards behind me, and John will follow you. If we run into a roadblock, stay back. I suspect we will run into another one manned by a remaining gang member. Now that we know that the additional people's weapons are props, we can focus on the one out front. Any questions before we head out?"

"No. I understand. We'll keep our eyes peeled for any trouble along the way."

I gave the command to Ruffus to load up, and he climbed into the backseat of the Jeep. When Claire hopped in, he put his head on her shoulder and licked her cheek.

I put the Jeep into gear, and we headed out.

A few miles down the road, we hit another roadblock.

One of the men stepped forward, grinning.

Ruffus, standing between Claire and me, growled at the thug, showing his displeasure.

I slowed down, pulled my pistol, and kept it below the window until I was about ten feet from the thug. I fired a single round left-handed. The back of his skull split open as the bullet passed through, and his body folded to the pavement, and I brought the Jeep to a stop.

The others dropped their rifles and raised their hands, yelling, "Don't shoot, don't shoot."

I climbed out of my Jeep to talk to them. "You're free to go. We cleared their camp. There were women and kids—we sent them home. Go home, arm yourselves. Protect your families."

"Thank you," a few of them mumbled.

"No problem, any chance you can help us clear the road of these vehicles?"

"No problem," one of the younger guys said.

We pushed both vehicles to the side of the road and out of our way.

As I climbed back into the Jeep, I called back to them, "Thanks for the help. Remember what I said."

Then we were back on Highway 88, southbound.

Headed home.

Chapter 7

When the Coffee Dies

Mel

I woke up missing TJ—and our ridiculous dog, Ruffus—but I had the entire king-size bed to myself, which let me stretch out like a lazy cat. The early sun had already crested the horizon, warming the hills and spreading golden light across the ranch. I loved this place. Our home. Our haven. Shelly and I were holding down the fort while our guys were off on one of their Rubicon Trail excursions. It was one of their favorite escapes—Jeep, trail, tools, and zero cell service.

They'd planned three full days on the trail. I imagined them crawling over granite, working on sections of the path, and relaxing at camp with beers in hand. They'd spent years volunteering their time to maintain the Rubicon. I was proud of them both.

I threw back the covers and swung my legs over the edge of the bed. The floor was cold under my feet, so I made my way quickly to the shower, the cold sinking into my feet with each step. The blast of hot water hit my skin, and I stood there for a moment, letting the heat soak in. After a moment, I grabbed the soap, lathering myself up, before rinsing and getting out of the shower. I toweled off and got dressed. I walked past Shelly's room on my way to the kitchen. Hearing her footsteps as she neared the door, I turned back to face it and waited. When she opened it, I shouted, "Boo!"

She screamed and fumbled her water bottle. "Oh, shit! Don't do that to a girl so early. I about keeled over," she gasped, holding her hand to her heart.

I grinned. "Bet your heart's racing now. You're ready for the day."

She slugged my arm. "It was already beating—before you tried to kill me."

I laughed with her as we wandered into the kitchen.

"I wonder if the boys are enjoying themselves up there," I said.

Shelly rolled her eyes. "As long as they can sit around, drink, and scratch themselves without us yelling at them, they're having a great time."

"Fair point."

I hit the button on our new Keurig to start the coffee brewing. Nothing happened.

"Really?" I muttered. "We just bought this thing." I glared at it. "Guess I'll break out TJ's old percolator. He always says it makes 'chewy coffee.'"

"Nah," Shelly said. "Let's run into town. There's that new coffee shop we passed the other day. It looked cute. I'll buy."

"Sold. Let me grab my keys."

Shutting the door to the house, we went down the steps of the porch and headed out to my truck. I pressed the key fob. No lights. No locks. Nothing.

I tried it again, still nothing.

"Battery's probably dead," I muttered. "First the coffee pot, now the truck."

I pulled out the physical key, opened the door, and noticed the interior light didn't come on. When I turned the ignition, the engine didn't even click.

"Great," I groaned. "Totally dead. I don't even know where

the jumper cables are."

I reached into my purse for my phone and tapped the screen. Dead.

I stared at it. "It was charging all night."

"Try yours," I said to Shelly.

She pulled out her phone and pressed the power button. Nothing.

"Mine's dead too," she said. "Damn. You think ... this is it? The guys are always talking about the shit hitting the fan. Is this that?"

I exhaled slowly. "Could be. But why do the lights and water still work in the house?"

"Well," she said, "the guys spent a lot of money EMP-proofing the house. Maybe all the shielding worked, except for your coffee pot. I think TJ said we'd still have some stuff that ran off the backup systems."

I nodded. "Could've at least saved the Keurig," I grumbled. "Do you think the guys know what happened? Will they come back early?"

Shelly raised her shoulders in a shrug. "If they figured it out, they're already on their way."

I turned back toward the house. "Guess we're making coffee the old-fashioned way."

As we reached the steps, a roaring engine echoed across the field. Dust kicked up from behind Joe's ATV as he sped toward us, leaving a long tan cloud in his wake.

He skidded to a stop, coughing into the dust cloud he'd dragged along.

"Morning, ladies," he said. "I'm guessing you figured out something's wrong. Looks like a full system failure. Nothing newer than a carburetor works."

"Good morning, Joey," I said. "Yeah, we figured it out when the Keurig wouldn't start, the truck wouldn't unlock, and both of our phones were bricks. TJ's always said if the shit ever hit the fan, we'd know it. And here we are."

Joe gave a lopsided grin. "Well, you've got food, power, and a solid roof. We're better off than most. But grab your weapons. If folks out there realize what's happened, some won't take it well."

"True. Come inside. I'll make some chewy coffee," I said.

Joe chuckled. "Not sure if it's chewy from the grounds or because you can stand a spoon up in it."

"Probably both."

"You know what?" he said. "I'll sit on the porch and watch the morning roll in."

"Suit yourself."

I went inside, fired up the gas stove, and loaded the percolator. At least the battery backup system still powered the essentials. While the coffee brewed, I found some breakfast bars and took them outside for Joe and Shelly, then returned to keep an eye on the percolator cap, watching the water darken.

Once the color looked right, I poured three cups and stepped out into the sunlight.

"Here you go. I hope it's not too weak—or too chewy."

Joe took a sip and sighed. "Perfect, Mel."

Shelly sipped hers and asked, "So … what do we do today, now that the world's gone to hell?"

"We prep," Joe answered. "Lock things down, check the supplies, stay ready. Don't wait for trouble—prepare for it."

"I'll pull something out for lunch and dinner," I said. "Any requests?"

"Meatloaf," Joe said immediately. "I haven't had your meatloaf in forever."

"Done. I've got ham and fixings for sandwiches, too."

We sat there, sipping coffee. I watched the breeze roll through the grass, and hoped our men were smart enough to realize what had happened—and were already on their way home.

Chapter 8

First Ripples

Late afternoon, the warmth of the day turned heavy. It clung to my skin, making everything feel slower than it should've. I'd prepped meatloaf for dinner and had it resting on the counter, ready to go into the oven. The house was quiet—too quiet. Even the birds seemed uneasy.

I was in the pantry with Shelly, reorganizing shelves and checking expiration dates, when Joe walked in the back door.

"Hey," he said, his voice low. "Might want to come see this."

We followed him out onto the covered back deck, where the spotting scope sat mounted on a tripod. It was aimed at the ridge road about a mile off, normally used by ranchers and off-roaders who knew the back ways into the valley.

I peered through the lens. Two figures moved along the road. They weren't hiking. They were searching. I watched them rifle through an overturned SUV that looked like it had rolled off the gravel shoulder. One of the men had a machete hanging from his belt. The other carried what looked like a crowbar. Neither looked friendly.

"Looters?" I asked, my voice tight. "I wonder where the people from the SUV went."

Joe nodded, considering the situation. "Maybe. Or just opportunists," he said thoughtfully, his gaze lingering on the distant figures. He kept his voice low, the tension clear. "But that's the third group I've seen on that ridge since noon."

He gestured toward the wrecked SUV visible through the

spotting scope. "The wreck doesn't look bad, and they could have walked back to their house or headed down the road towards town. They probably crashed when the power went out during the event, killing the engine and electronics."

Shelly stepped forward. "Any of them heading this way?"

"Not yet. But they're moving slowly. Scouting, probably."

I swallowed and looked toward the barn, where the perimeter alarm cables ran into the soil and fence line. I thought about the system TJ had installed with Joe's help, low-voltage trip lines buried beneath gravel and disguised along key entry routes. It wouldn't stop anyone, but it would give us time to react.

"Should we set the trip alarms to live?" I asked.

Joe nodded. "I was just about to suggest it."

"I'll handle the east and north fences, Shelly. Can you check the greenhouse doors and the fuel storage? Make sure they're locked and secure."

"On it," she said, already moving.

Joe grabbed his rifle, leaned against the porch wall, and checked the action to verify a round was chambered. "I'll watch the ridge."

My boots crunched over the gravel as I walked the perimeter, pulling the trip line toggles into the "armed" position. Each click reminded me how quickly life had changed—from morning coffee to lockdown measures in a single day. I checked the water storage tank behind the greenhouse, then headed toward the livestock barn to make sure the feed room door was locked.

When I circled back to the front porch, Joe was still at the scope. He looked up and gave a slow shake of his head.

"They're gone," he said. "Ducked down the other side of the ridge. Might've just been scavenging. But I don't like it."

"Me neither."

A beat of silence passed.

I gave Joe a long look. "You think TJ and John ran into anything worse?"

"I think they're smart. They'll come back the second they realize what's going on."

"They'd better."

Shelly returned from the other side of the property. "Everything's locked down. Fuel tanks are good. Greenhouse doors are secure."

"Let's keep one person on watch until sundown," Joe said. "Rotate every hour. If anything feels wrong, ring the bell."

We all turned to look at the old school bell mounted near the back door. TJ had installed it for emergencies—one loud clang to bring everyone running. I never thought we'd actually need it.

"I'll take first watch," I offered. "You two relax for a bit."

Joe nodded, and Shelly squeezed my shoulder before heading inside.

I sat on the porch, wishing that Ruffus were beside me. His ears and eyes were so much better than mine.

The ripple had started. And soon, the wave would come crashing in.

Chapter 9

Ranch Reunites

TJ

As I approached the back gate, I looked at my indicator light in the brush to see if Mel had armed the trip sensors. If you knew where to look, there was a small light indicating that the system was on. *Smart, Mel*, I said to myself. Clearing the back gate, the house came into view as we approached the ranch—solid, familiar, and comforting. Mel and Shelly stood on the wrap-around porch, arms crossed but faces full of relief.

I brought the Jeep to a stop and climbed out. Mel sauntered down the steps, her hips swaying.

"Hey sailor," she said with a grin. "Looking for a good time? Cheap, cheap. I take good care of you."

I smirked. "Sure thing, missy. How much? Are you any good?"

"Me plenty good, and cheap. Don't clean house, but me take care of you plenty," she teased.

Her eyes flicked past me to the new faces.

"Who are your new friends? You find a new girl on the trail? Gonna replace me?"

I shook my head. "Could never replace you, sweetheart. These two are Tracy and Claire. We found them near Cadillac Hill— rescued them from a couple of dirtbags. They're nurses. Saw what was happening and decided to join us."

I gestured behind me. "This is Billy, his wife Joanne, and their kids, Melissa and Charlie. They had it rough, but they're good people. Let's show them the bunkhouse so they can settle in. Everyone's probably starving."

John and I took turns explaining what had happened while we were gone.

Mel and I headed to the bunkhouse with our new crew. "How's the house holding up now that everything's dead?"

She shrugged. "Didn't even realize anything was wrong at first. I tried to make coffee this morning, but the Keurig wouldn't turn on. The truck wouldn't unlock, wouldn't start. Phones are dead. But the lights, water, and everything else inside the house worked just like you said they would. Shelly's truck still runs. Mine doesn't."

I nodded. "Good to know the EMP shielding worked. And yes … this is it. The end of the world as we knew it. TEOTWAWKI. From now on, we'll tighten security, find like-minded people, and protect this place. The front fence is solid. The river on the west gives us water. But the back line is still too open. We'll need to address that."

Ruffus sprinted past me, chasing one of his old tennis balls. Charlie was throwing it with a laugh. Ruffus was already hooked on him.

"Let's get everyone settled," I said, "then we eat."

We showed our new guests the bunkhouse, pointing out its features. "As you can see, each room is set up the same. A large commercial kitchen is available here, and there are two large tables for dining. You all can pick your rooms," I said.

"Wow, nice place," Tracy said.

Charlie was running into each room, with Ruffus close on his heels.

"We will need to find some bunk beds. I'm sure we will

increase the size of our family, and not everyone will want to share a bed," I said as I looked at Charlie and Melissa.

"Yeah, I don't like sleeping with girls," Charlie said, and looked at his sister with his brows furrowed.

"I don't like sleeping with boys either. They stink, and he snores," she said as she plugged her nose with two fingers.

I laughed at their brotherly and sisterly antics. *Oh, to be young again.* "Pick your rooms out. We can unload the trailers after we eat.

"You still making meatloaf?" Joe asked, interrupting our tour

"Yes, Joe," Mel said. "I'm making three pans now that we've got a full house."

"Can I have my own room?" Charlie asked.

"For now," I replied. "But if or when we get more people, you'll probably have a bunkmate."

"What do you use this for?" Joanne asked as she continued to look around the dining area.

"Great question. As you can see, we have ten rooms, each with a queen bed. We originally built it for training groups. John and I used to teach tactical weapons courses here on weekends. It also has a full kitchen for feeding the teams we trained. It kept everyone out of the house."

"It's great. How did you ever find this place?" Billy asked.

"After I retired, we looked around and happened to meet the original owner. We became fast friends over the years. He and his wife had no kids to give it to, so we would often come out and help them around the place. We were just trying to be nice and kind. One day, they offered to sell us the ranch for a price that we couldn't turn down. Part of the deal included them staying here until they passed. We agreed. Mel had her prepper blog up and running, and she was making a good income from it. We researched how to make an EMP-proof shop," I said as I looked around the room. "I met John on the Rubicon, found out he did weapons training, along with my competitive shooting skills, we built the range and started holding training courses. Every weekend was booked, and training with local law enforcement during the week. We've done well here. Not that it matters now."

"Let's check the shop. I want to confirm everything's still running as it should be," I said to John.

We walked over, unlocked the door, and flipped on the lights. The overhead fluorescents blinked once and then came alive.

"All good," I said. "Server lights are still blinking. Solar system looks fine."

I pulled a backup laptop from the equipment cage, opened the lid, and hit the power button; it powered up. The startup screen loaded like normal.

"Our optics still worked on the Rubicon. Radios were dead, but the sights didn't flicker. Glad we spent the money on military grade optics," I said

"They cost a fortune but are worth every penny."

We walked back across the yard. My stomach growled like a diesel engine. John looked over at me. "Hungry?"

I gave him a sheepish look. "I could eat a horse. Let's round everyone up. Mel should be just about done."

We entered the bunkhouse. Everyone was lounging around the table. Charlie and Ruffus lay sprawled out together on the floor. I looked down at Ruffus.

"Traitor," I mouthed.

"Dinner ready?" someone asked.

"Let's go—single file," I said, and grinned. "Stay in step. Left, your left, right, left," I called out like I was marching them to a chow hall.

"Not heard that in forever," Billy said, grinning ear to ear.

We crossed the yard, and as we stepped inside, the smell hit me—Mel's spaghetti, garlic, tomato, meat, herbs. Heaven. Crossing into the kitchen, my stomach growled again, and Mel smirked at me.

"Oh yeah," I said. "How long?"

Mel strained the noodles. "Five, maybe ten minutes. Meatloaf's almost done, too."

"Hey John, grab a bottle of wine from the cooler," I said. "I'll show our guests the house."

"Hey, everyone. I'll give you the dime tour while we wait for dinner," I said.

"What's a dime tour?" Charlie asked with a sheepish grin.

"It's what I have to charge you for the tour of the house," I said, grinning. The term and meaning came from the old dime stores and dime novels, that someone was getting over giving a quick or informal tour," I replied.

"Oh, I don't have a dime," Charlie said.

"No problem, Charlie. I'm not really going to charge you for the tour. You saw the kitchen there, the living room here, the spare bedrooms down here, our room is upstairs, along with a game room. We don't really have any games in it, though," I said. "There is a basement with storage with stuff we have stockpiled, in case of an event like this."

Back in the kitchen, Shelly was spooning meat into one bowl and tomato sauce into another.

Melissa tilted her head. "Why don't you mix them?"

"Mel doesn't eat meat," Shelly replied. "So, we keep it separate."

Melissa turned to Mel. "Why don't you eat meat?"

"Bad experience as a kid," Mel said. "Haven't touched it since."

"Mom, can I stop eating meat, too?" Melissa asked.

Joanne raised an eyebrow. "If you want. I'd prefer you eat it—for the nutrients."

Charlie cut in. "Let her stop. More steak for me."

Joanne rolled her eyes.

"Hey, Mel," I said. "Seen Joe today?"

She nodded. "He came by this morning to check on us after everything went down. He went home for a little bit just before you all arrived. You know Joe—he'll show up when dinner's almost ready."

Right on cue, the rumble of an ATV rolled across the field in a cloud of dust. Joe pulled up, parked, and marched into the house like he owned the place.

"Evening, kids. What's for dinner?"

"Crayons," I said with a straight face. "We're out of red, though. Somebody already ate 'em."

Joe smirked. "Damn. Those are my favorites."

Charlie poked his head around the corner. "Why do you eat crayons?"

Joe stopped mid-step, looked at him, and chuckled. "It's just a joke, kid. Marines and crayons. Long story. Who are the new people?" he asked.

Charlie nodded like he totally understood. "Okay."

"We're having spaghetti and meatloaf," I said and made the introductions.

When I introduced Claire and Tracy, he grabbed their hands

with both of his and bowed. "What lovely ladies you are," he said.

"Your dad is so nice," Claire said and chuckled.

"He's not my father, though we treat him like a father, though. He is our cranky, Marine neighbor who we love."

Joe grinned. "That's more like it, though I knew of the meatloaf."

He'd been a neighbor and close friend for years. Retired Marine Gunnery Sergeant. Tough as nails. At sixty-seven, he was still solid muscle and sharper than most men half his age. We always joked about the Navy and Marine rivalry, but we'd fight beside him without hesitation.

Mel called out. "Grab the plates and silverware, love. Dinner's nearly ready."

I pulled the plates out of the cupboard. "C'mon, everyone, dinner's nearly ready. Come and sit at the table." I grabbed the silverware and placed it on the top plate. Walking to the table, I popped them down as Mel and Shelly walked over with spaghetti and meatloaf.

Dishing up food onto my plate, I looked around the table. Everyone's plates were full of food, and the faint lines of tension had eased from their faces.

"You all settled in?" I asked.

Joanne smiled. "The rooms are great."

Tracy and Claire nodded, their mouths full.

I glanced at Mel. We had come a long way in preparing this place. The basement was packed with supplies—canned food, dehydrated produce, ammo, and medical gear. The freeze-dryer and dehydrator were still humming, working through the last harvest.

The shop housed equipment, tools, and my reloading bench.

The armory held our reserve weapons and spare parts. We'd built it to weather a storm.

Now the storm was here.

And we were ready.

Chapter 10

Building the New Tribe

After dinner, John, Shelly, Mel, and I gathered in the living room to talk. The kids were tucked away, and the bunkhouse had gone quiet. I could still smell the spaghetti and meatloaf hanging in the air, but my thoughts had shifted to what came next.

"We all agree this was an EMP, right?"

Everyone nodded.

"We need to start expanding the ranch family. Carefully. We'll need people with practical skills—and the right attitude—to help us survive long-term." I grabbed a notebook and uncapped a pen. "Let's list out the people and skill sets we want to bring in."

John chuckled. "Here comes the monkey list."

Mel raised an eyebrow. "Monkey list?"

"He means problem-solving," I said. "Write them all down like monkeys on branches. Knock 'em off one by one."

"Law enforcement or military," Mel started.

"A doctor or someone with strong medical training," Shelly added.

"We've got Claire and Tracy," I reminded them. "They're trauma nurses, which gives us a strong start. But we'll need a vetting process. We don't just let anyone walk in. Rule one: contribute. Rule two: don't be an ass."

"How are we going to vet people with no internet and Google?" Mel asked, arching an eyebrow at me.

"I hope that someone knows them and can vouch for them.

If not, we must take their word for it until they prove otherwise," I said, and sighed. "This team will have the final say on whether we have to kick someone out. If we do kick someone out, it could be a death sentence for them in the world outside our fence."

"True," Shelly replied.

John brought us back to the task at hand. "What's our ideal headcount?"

I frowned. "Hard to say. Enough to sustain defense, grow food, and rotate shifts without burning out. We need a cook—or chef—who understands nutrition and can run the kitchen. Also, we'll hit a housing limit soon. Ten rooms in the bunkhouse. We'll need overflow options."

"I can increase the garden output," Mel said. "With help, we can expand production and preserve everything we grow."

"And we still have plenty of greenhouse space," Shelly added. "If we bring in someone to help full-time, maybe another gardener or a master grower, we could really ramp up yield."

The greenhouse measured thirty by sixty feet and sat adjacent to the shop.

Mel nodded. "With that woodstove, it will be able to run year-round. The herb section I started, featuring tea plants, medicinal varieties, and heirloom vegetables, will be invaluable. The small orchard and nut grove at the back edge of our land will help us get our nutrients."

"We'll need to get back to our house soon," John said. "I've got long-term food storage and some weapons stored there, and I don't want someone breaking into it."

"We'll head there tomorrow," I replied. "Shelly's truck can tow the trailer. We'll make it quick."

"We should ask Joe if he knows any good people to bring in," I suggested. "Between our 2,000 acres and his 1,000, we'll need help—and soon."

"Don't forget the local nurseries," Mel said. "The trees there will die without care. We could rescue them."

"And trade excess produce," I added. "Turn our surplus into a barter system."

We then discussed water storage and filtration, including a solar-powered well, gravity-fed creek access, and 500-gallon tanks ready for backup storage.

By the time we wrapped the discussion, it was pushing twenty-two hundred. Everyone was ready for bed.

Shelly gave John a look that made it clear they were heading off to their side of the house for a different kind of strategy meeting.

"You two keep it down," I teased.

Chapter 11

First Light, First Threat

I woke up at zero six hundred, and the smell of crisp air and pine drifted through the bedroom window. I brewed a pot of coffee on the gas stove and listened to the percolator rattle to life.

The house was still. I couldn't hear anyone moving yet. I sat on the porch with my second cup and watched the sun claw its way over the eastern Nevada hills. That glow warmed my soul like nothing else. About fifteen minutes later, I heard footsteps inside, and then the front door opened. John sat down beside me, a coffee in his hand.

A few minutes later, Mel and Shelly stepped out onto the porch, wrapped in jackets, their cups steaming. We all sat in silence, watching the world wake up.

Ruffus had followed Mel and Shelly out and had come to sit beside me, his head resting on my knee.

Then he stiffened. His ears perked, and a deep growl rumbled in his throat.

"What is it, boy?" I asked.

He chuffed, his eyes locked on the shop.

John scrambled to his feet. "Shit. We're unarmed."

I stood. "Ruffus, protect. John, there are two rifles by the front door—I'll grab them."

"Got it," he said, already moving.

"Ladies, inside and strap up. Stay alert."

Picking up the rifles from just inside the front door, I stepped back onto the porch, handing one to John, and then I racked the action on my rifle. John followed close behind. Ruffus was glued to my left side, a low growl rising again as we approached the shop.

"Could be a curious guest," John muttered.

"Probably not," I replied. "Ruffus doesn't growl at deer."

Fifty feet from the shop, a figure moved in the shadows, trying to duck away.

I snapped my Surefire light on.

"Stop right there!" I barked. "Hands up, or I'll release the dog!"

Ruffus barked once, sharp and harsh, his hackles raised.

Mel's voice echoed from the porch. "Ladies are back and armed. Don't make us come down there!"

The man froze, hands trembling.

"I-I was just looking for food," he stammered. "The stores in town were raided. They're only taking cash. No one's cards work."

"And your answer is sneaking onto someone else's land?" I snapped. "If you'd just knocked, maybe we could've helped."

"John, search him," I added. "You run, I'll turn the dog loose after you. He hasn't eaten yet."

Ruffus growled, just to underscore the point.

"I saw the dog," the guy mumbled, his shoulders slumped. "I don't like dogs."

Ruffus barked again, louder. The man flinched hard, and I saw a wet patch begin in his crotch and work its way down his legs. John and I chuckled under our breath.

"I'm not going to shoot you," I said. "But if you ever come back uninvited, you'll stay here—permanently."

I pointed down the driveway. "Now go."

He stumbled off down the driveway, his feet scuffing the dirt.

I turned to John as we made our way to the porch, with glances toward our retreating intruder. "We need to start setting up cameras and perimeter sensors around the front gate. No more surprises."

"Agreed. You've got the gear?"

"Twenty cameras. Thirty sensors. Some thermal. Some wireless. Some hardwired. Everything's pre-configured and solar compatible."

"We'll need to divide the property into sectors and wire zones," John replied. "Prioritize the weak points."

Back on the porch, Mel and Shelly were standing in their tactical gear, rifles slung over the shoulders.

"Might need a detour to the bedroom before breakfast," I said to Mel.

She gave me a sly grin. "Later. Right now, you've got bacon and eggs waiting."

"I'll take it."

I rang the triangle bell outside the bunkhouse, letting it chime through the cool morning.

"Y'all look like you lost a fight with your pillow," I said as I watched Claire and Tracy shuffle out of the bunkhouse first, their hair sticking up at all angles.

"What in Sam hell is that noise?" Tracy grumbled.

"Breakfast," I said. "Up and at 'em."

Billy and Joanne emerged a moment later, their hair equally wild.

"Next time, show me the snooze button," Billy muttered.

"Be in the house in ten," I said, already walking away.

As breakfast wrapped up, I gave the group their marching orders.

"Here's the plan. We'll retrieve John and Shelly's gear

tomorrow. Today, we arm everyone and prep defenses. Adults must carry at all times. If you don't have weapons, we'll outfit you. Claire, Tracy—check your loads. Kids, too, if Billy and Joanne approve."

Melissa raised her hand. "We've both been trained."

Her parents nodded.

"Then you're both on the roster," I said. "We'll run everyone through the range today."

Walking over to the shop, John and I led the group to the big steel doors, creaking them open to reveal the expanse inside.

Their eyes went wide.

"First stop: gear up," I said. "Grab what you brought. The rest, we'll outfit here."

While the group backtracked to the bunkhouse, John and I reviewed the ham radio setup and security system. He nodded toward the gear.

"Shop or bunkhouse?"

"Bunkhouse. Faster alerts. Closer to the people."

Mel strolled in as I pulled boxes down.

"What is all this?" she asked.

"Security cameras. Sensors. Radios."

"When did you buy all this?"

"Umm … before. Probably didn't tell you."

She crossed her arms. "Communication, mister."

Joe rolled up on his ATV, dust flying. "You're in trouble," he laughed.

"Always am," I replied.

"First, you're late for breakfast. We had an intruder this morning looking for food. Ruffus keyed up on his arrival. I'm grabbing the cameras and sensors for the security system. We might want to find a chef and see if he or she would like to be a nutritionist."

"Had an issue with my ATV starting this morning. I'll reach out to a chef I know, and his family," Joe said. "And a couple of Marines and deputies."

"Make sure they know our rules: be useful, be kind, or be gone."

Joe nodded. "Got it. I'll be back by nightfall."

As he pulled away, John stood beside me, scratching his chin.

"You look like you've got something on your mind," I said.

"I've trained most of the local deputies. If they're still thinking straight, they'll come to us."

"I hope so, because this world isn't waiting for anyone to catch up."

Chapter 12

Contact on the Fence Line

Heading back toward the house, multiple sharp cracks split the air. Gunfire. It was close, near the road. Instinct took over.

We started scrambling for cover to figure out where the shooter or possible shooters were. "Kids, inside. Move," I shouted. From the sound of the shot, it was not aimed in our direction, though we weren't going to take any chances.

John yelled, "I think the shot came from the road, and sounded like a handgun."

So much for hitting the range before lunch, I thought.

"John, Shelly—cover that corner. Tracy and Claire, post near Mel's truck. Billy and Joanne— opposite side of the house."

I pointed to Ruffus and then to the retreating kids. "Protect."

He shot me a look, ears low—he hated being left out of the action—but turned and herded them inside.

"Mel, with me. We'll move to the east side for a better view of the road."

Joe tore up the drive on his ATV, dust rolling off his tires. He coughed through the cloud and shouted, "The deputies were headed this way when a gang tailed and ambushed them. Their truck's disabled. One of them made it to my place to alert me. They're pinned down and need help!"

John and I ran for his Jeep. I hadn't even shut my door before John threw the Jeep into gear. The wheels bit into the gravel, and we jolted forward, gravel spraying out behind us. We tore down the drive and along the fence line, the sound of bullets ringing out, before we had even reached the tree line.

Reaching the fence line along the road, John pulled us to a stop, and we jumped out of the Jeep. We hopped over the fence and dropped into the woods for cover. Working our way parallel to the road, I could see the gang; there were a handful of punks in white tees, jeans, and red bandanas. Vans on their feet. Classic thug starter kit.

Joe rolled up on the far side of the road, alongside the deputy who had made it to him.

John tapped my arm and motioned forward.

I eased carefully through the underbrush, and ducked under a low hanging branch, its leaves brushing my face. One of them, looking like he was in his mid-twenties, was holding his pistol sideways and fired rounds toward the deputies. I shook my head. *Who the hell holds their pistol like that and expects to hit anything?*

I leveled my rifle, centered the red dot on his chest, clicked the safety off, and squeezed. The rifle barked, a sudden, forceful shove into my shoulder. I rode the recoil and sight picture back to the target, and saw a red mist puff from his chest as he dropped. The blood ran out of his body in seconds.

To my right, John engaged. I could tell by the rhythm and discipline of his shots that his targets were going down fast.

The gang had pistols and shotguns. The deputies, thankfully, were using ARs—giving them better firepower.

I pushed forward, flanking left. A thug raised his shotgun over the trunk of a rusted-out Pontiac as I crept into position. I put my red dot on the center of his forehead and squeezed the trigger. His head snapped back, and his body crumpled out of view.

Across the road, Joe's M1 Garand barked—its .30-06 report like thunder. He worked the old rifle with calm precision. With iron sights and raw muscle memory, his ability to make hits from that distance blew me away.

At least four were down. A few more were still firing, but their aggression was fading.

Bark suddenly exploded near my face. Someone had spotted me. I ducked just as I heard Joe answer with another double-tap. The threat went silent.

John appeared at my flank, signaling we move north. We leapfrogged through the trees until we spotted two more thugs holding position behind the trunk of their Pontiac.

John signaled silently—three fingers down. On one, we fired.

Two shots. Two clouds of gray matter splattered the road behind them.

A final gang member bolted, sprinting down the centerline, away from the carnage.

Joe stepped up, cool as ever. "One of you going to finish that, or should I?"

Neither of us answered fast enough. Joe raised his Garand, sighted, and dropped the runner with a single shot from 200 yards out.

"You nitwits," he growled. "You let that bastard run, and he comes back with twenty more. No quarter in this world. None."

"You're right," I said.

John stared out over the aftermath, his expression weary. "This wasn't the world we'd known," he said, voice heavy with resignation.

The violence and loss, so far removed from the lives we'd once lived, weighed on us all.

John's sigh lingered in the air, a quiet acknowledgment of

how much everything had changed and of the grim reality they now faced together.

Chapter 13

Deputies and Decisions

As we walked toward the deputies' position, they stepped out from behind the trees they had been using as cover, weapons still shouldered. They recognized Joe immediately. A few nodded to John.

"Appreciate the backup," one said. "We'd be toast if you hadn't shown up."

Inspecting the bodies, I could see that there were five dead and one still breathing. That wouldn't be for long. His blood pumped out fast, spreading in a dark pool beneath him.

"We need to check their vehicle and yours. There might be something worth salvaging." I knew all the deputies. They had trained at our range a while back. Matthew and Russell had families in town.

"We were headed to Joe's to see if we could relocate out here," Matthew said.

"Looks like the dirtbags got a lucky shot into your rear tire. We can find one and get you all to Joe's or our ranch," I said as I inspected their flat tire.

"I believe I've got a spare rim and tire for that truck back at my shop," Joe said.

Matthew nodded. "I would appreciate that."

Joe moved towards the gang's low rider. "Let's see if this thing even runs." He twisted the key. The Pontiac sputtered to life but shook violently, smoke rolling out from under the hood. He cut it off. "Dead soon anyway."

"Let's drag the bodies off the road," I said. "The coyotes have to eat too."

Joe and a few deputies got to work.

"Are you all still active?" I asked while we worked.

"Nope. The sheriff told us to take our gear and go protect our families. Phones are dead. No 911," Matthew replied, his voice steady but tired.

"It's not good in town," Russell said, through tired, bloodshot eyes. "There's a gang in town now. Leader's the sheriff's kid," Dylan said. "We tried to arrest him once—he was back on the street before I'd finished the paperwork."

"Great," I muttered.

"TJ," Matthew added. "My daughter's name is Isabella. She and Bonnie trained at your range. You helped them prep for those competitions."

I smiled. "Good kids. Fast learners. They'd go far."

We gathered the weapons from the dead and loaded them into the deputies' truck.

Cole drove their truck to Joe's with the flat. John and I followed the fence line back in the Jeep, this time driving at a more sedate pace.

"Drop me at Joe's," I said. "Grab Shelly's truck and the trailer—we'll start relocating the families."

By the time I arrived at Joe's place, they were unloading gear. I climbed out of the Jeep. "Hey, folks. John's heading out to get the trailer. Once he's back, we'll split up, grab your stuff, and get everyone settled. Just the essentials—clothes, weapons, food, and if the kids have bikes or toys, pack those too."

"Who's doing the cooking?" Cole asked.

Madison snorted. "Not me. You're grown. Cook for yourselves. I've seen your sad lunches—you'll all starve."

Joe laughed. "I'll talk to the folks at C's Fine Dining. He and his family would be perfect here. Bunkhouse kitchen's solid, and he can run the show."

Dylan looked around. "Sounds like it's TJ's ranch, then."

Everyone nodded in agreement.

John pulled up in the truck and trailer.

"Where to first?"

"Let's split up," I said. "Each of you takes a family. The rest provide security. No furniture—just the basics."

Joe rolled out his own truck and trailer. Each family jumped into a separate truck.

"See you soon," I called as they rolled down the drive.

I felt conflicted. We had new blood and a growing network, but we also had new threats. This was just the beginning.

Chapter 14

Secrets beneath the Surface

Calling over the handheld, I gave the all-clear. "Stand down from perimeter detail, everyone. The situation is contained."

I headed back to the ranch at a leisurely pace, walking across the field. Twenty minutes later, walking up to the porch, Mel met me, brow furrowed. "What was all that shooting?"

"Deputies from the sheriff's office showed up," I said. "They wanted to know if they could relocate here. The sheriff cut everyone loose—no pay, no working vehicles, no way to communicate. Total collapse. We told them they're welcome. Right now, they're at Joe's unloading the captured weapons and looking for a replacement tire for their truck."

Shelly joined us, brushing dust from her pants. "What's left in the shop for today?"

"It's almost lunchtime," Mel interjected. "Let's head inside and make soup and sandwiches. We've got enough to feed the deputies, too, if they make it here in time."

"Two of them have families. The bunkhouse should fit them all," I added. "Joe also mentioned a chef in town with a wife and kids, as well as a couple of former Marines. If they agree to come, the bunkhouse will be full."

The team headed back into the house to prepare lunch, the sound of their chatter fading as they closed the front door behind them. Lingering for a moment, I then headed over to the shop where I began unloading more security gear—tactical vests with plates, bump helmets, and night vision goggles. *We're not prepping anymore, we're ready for a fight.* My stomach flipped as the reality of the situation sank in.

John arrived, his truck crunching on the gravel as he parked in front of the bunkhouse. Hopping out, we both took the families inside the bunkhouse to show them their new living quarters.

"Hey, John. I've got something cool to show you at the shop—but this is eyes-only. No one else gets to know."

He raised a brow. "What are you dragging me into now?"

I walked into the armory in the shop, with John close behind. "See that button on the wall? Push it, then grab the back corner of the desk and pull."

He frowned. "I'm not exactly in desk-lifting shape."

"Just do it."

He pressed the button, and with a soft click, the heavy oak desk shifted away from the wall. When he tugged the corner, the desk slid free, revealing a tunnel entrance descending into darkness.

"What. In. The. Hell." His voice echoed slightly off the concrete walls.

"Head on down."

"You're not going to kill me down there, are you?" he joked, half serious.

"Not unless you break into my liquor stash," I said, and smacked him on the shoulder.

The tunnel was cool and slightly damp as we descended. I reached over and flipped on a switch. LED lights buzzed to life overhead, illuminating wide shelves lining the walls—supplies stacked floor to ceiling.

"This is our underground storage and utility tunnel," I said. "Mel keeps an inventory of everything down here. Medical supplies, long-term food, emergency equipment … you name it. All the main power and utility lines run through here from the shop to the house."

John's jaw dropped. "How long is this thing?"

"Just under three hundred feet. It runs from the shop to the root cellar in the basement. We added ventilation to keep it dry. I need to reset the fans to prevent moisture from getting to the food. Oh, and keep an eye out—we also use this for wine and liquor storage. You'll see the collection as we get closer to the house."

He looked around, his mouth ajar. "Holy shit, dude, this must've cost a fortune."

I chuckled. "It wasn't cheap, but it was worth every cent. In bad weather or during an attack, this gives us a backdoor route to flank anyone trying to breach the house."

As we reached the exit into the root cellar, John still looked stunned.

Climbing the stairs, we walked into the kitchen from the basement door. Shelly spun around, startled.

"Where did you two come from? I didn't hear the front door."

Mel grinned as she stirred the pot on the stove. "I'll tell you later," she said with a wink. "Or maybe I'll show you."

Chapter 15

The Working Dog

Ruffus

The bed creaked.

I pushed up and stretched, my front paws out, tail high, then padded to the edge. TJ was coming back from his morning duties. I could hear his boots before he walked back into the room. Not just the sound—*the rhythm*. Solid. Familiar. Mine.

I knew his routine. He opened the door and headed down the stairs to the kitchen, where he would brew his coffee in the noisy pot, and I would head for the door with the flappy thing on it. I was right there with him and received a scratch on the top of my head. The familiar feeling of his hand on my head was always comforting.

I had my own routine. I ran outside and headed for my favorite tree. Stopping to check if we had any visitors during the night. Nope. I made my way around the front of the house and saw TJ step out onto the porch with a cup of black liquid that had a peculiar, burnt smell. I tried it once, and didn't like it. It was also very hot and burned my tongue.

He stepped outside with his rifle across his back and his coffee in hand.

"You ready for our morning walk, buddy?" TJ asked.

We didn't need words, though he said them every morning. I trotted ahead.

The gravel path crunched beneath my paws. Damp. It rained

last night. Air smelled of pine sap and the faint sweetness of the greenhouse. I paused at the junction near the barn and looked back. TJ nodded.

Walking the perimeter, I stayed thirty paces ahead of TJ, nose sweeping left and right, always scanning. There was a squirrel's trail—too fresh—and a patch where the fence-line wire had loosened just a little. I marked it with a low chuff, and TJ made his way over to check it.

At the north fence, he crouched. I held my position beside him, ears up. A branch had snapped nearby. I heard it first—soft, wrong, not wind.

I didn't bark.

Just stared.

Two deer emerged from the tree line, hooves light on the ridge gravel. I huffed. Not a threat.

TJ murmured, "Good job Ruffus." His voice meant calm. I let the tension go, shook out my coat.

We moved on.

At the creek line, he bent again, checking wires and strange plastic boxes that sometimes clicked. I didn't understand what they did, but they mattered. While he worked, I sat on the high rock and watched the west ridge. The wind shifted. I caught the scent of raccoon. Snake. And something else.

I have a little chuff to get TJ's attention, and put my nose to the ground, sniffing the impression in the soft dirt.

Boots. Human. Not one of ours.

My ears pressed forward.

I turned to see TJ already watching me.

TJ found the prints just like I had. I sat beside them, nose low, body still. He studied the tracks, then made marks in a little book he always carried. His hands smelled like ink and oil.

"I think we have someone watching our ranch," TJ said. "I need to have John set a trail camera out here."

We worked our way back to the house and breakfast. I played with the new little human, Charlie, after breakfast. I liked Charlie; he shared food with me at the table.

I followed TJ and Mel as they rearranged the space and brought boxes from the shop.

I had lunch with Charlie and then took a nap. All the running around watching my hoomans was tiring, and I had a full belly. Charlie again gave me a lot of his ham, as they called it. It was yummy, though not as good as bacon. I woke up from my nap when I heard gunshots from the range. I headed that way.

"Ruffus. Sit over here with Charlie," TJ commanded when I got close.

I sat with Charlie. He scratched behind my ears. *Good spot.*

He threw a stick. I fetched it.

Twice.

I didn't like this game. *Chewing on bad guys.* That was my favorite.

I lay down and placed my paw on the stick so he wouldn't throw it again. He laughed. I wagged my tail once.

Later, TJ gave a sharp whistle, and I bolted upright, quickly looked around for danger, and bound to his side, leaving Charlie sitting on the grass with the stick.

I was sitting with Mama Mel and TJ after dinner. I placed my head on TJ's leg. It was warm. Familiar. Safe.

His hand found the spot between my ears.

"Good boy, Ruffus," he said.

My tail wagged across the wooden porch, like it had a mind of its own, as TJ rubbed my head.

I chuffed in response, though I didn't need the words.

I already knew.

Chapter 16

New Faces, Old Tensions

TJ

I stepped into the bunkhouse and found Tracy, Claire, Billy, Joanne, and the kids chatting at the kitchen table.

"Hey, everyone. How's it going?" I asked.

"Pretty good," came a chorus of responses.

"I miss my phone and computer," Charlie muttered with a dramatic sigh.

"I bet you do, Charlie," I replied with a chuckle. "Honestly, I miss mine too … though maybe not as much as I thought I would."

I stepped further into the room. "I wanted to share some updates now that the world's gone sideways—SHTF, as we always talked about. We've got a few deputies coming out here soon. Joe's also rounding up a chef and a few Marines.

At the mention of Marines, Claire and Tracy perked up, eyes wide. I suppressed a grin.

Tracy asked, "How many people do you think you'll bring out here in total?"

I looked at Tracy. "Hard to say yet. The bunkhouse has ten rooms, each with a queen bed. We can add bunk beds to increase capacity. Our house has a couple of extra rooms, and Joe's place has some as well. Realistically, we can host forty people comfortably between all the buildings—for now."

Ruffus barked, moving to the door.

"Hold up, buddy," I said, reaching for my rifle as the familiar sound of an engine reached my ears.

Ruffus waited for me to reach him, then he flew out the door. I followed him to see Joe's truck pulling into the driveway, dust trailing behind him. Several passengers were with him. There was something familiar about the young woman sitting in the backseat.

Joe brought the truck to a stop, and everyone climbed out. Ruffus bounded toward them, tail wagging furiously, trying to sniff and say hello. The boy and the woman beside him both flinched when Ruffus came near.

The woman recoiled slightly. "Can you control your dog? He seems dangerous."

Before I could respond, Ruffus trotted over to the unfamiliar man next to her, sat in front of him, and lifted his paw in greeting.

Joe clapped the man on the back. "Everyone, come meet Clarence. Where's Mel?"

Mel walked out of the house with Shelly and John.

"I'm right here," Mel called. "Who've you brought us?"

Joe began introductions. "This is Clarence or Chef C, his wife Ann, and their kids—Bonnie and Brian." He looked toward the man beside him. "You probably know him from the restaurant in town. He's agreed to relocate here and manage the kitchen in exchange for a place to live."

I nodded, catching approving glances from Mel, John, and Shelly. "Welcome to Freedom Ranch," I said as I stepped forward to shake hands.

I recognized Clarence and his daughter from town. Bonnie had trained at the range and was one of the top youth shooters in the state.

"Hey, TJ!" Bonnie said. "I thought I recognized this place. Joe said we might stay here. I really hope so—your range is awesome."

Out of the corner of my eye, I saw her mother roll her eyes at the mention of guns.

Clarence stepped forward. "Thanks for having us. We're grateful. We'll contribute however we can."

As he spoke, Ann stood stiffly, arms crossed, her brow furrowed in clear disapproval.

Humm. I'll keep an eye on her, I said to myself.

"Our rules are simple," I told them. "Help out, don't be a jerk, and we all work together. That's how we survive."

"We heard gunfire in town last night," Clarence said. "It's going to get worse."

"I believe that too," I agreed. "We've got room now, but it'll fill up fast. The rooms all have queen beds, but we plan to check the furniture store in town for bunk beds. We're building a bigger group and a stronger defense."

"What else do you need?" Clarence asked. "We've still got food at the restaurant. If we move fast, we can save most of it."

"That'd be a big help. Once the deputies are settled, we'll get Joe and a crew to help haul the supplies."

Ann interjected sharply. "Do we really need to do all this? The power will come back on. The government will fix this."

"Mom—" Bonnie started.

"We're the most powerful country in the world," Ann continued, interrupting her daughter. "There's no way this lasts more than a few days. The government will fix everything."

I opened my mouth, but Mel gently elbowed me and gave me a warning glance.

Bonnie stepped up instead. "Mom, we learned about EMPs

in science. If that's what this was, it's going to take *years* to fix. This isn't just the power going out—it's the infrastructure breaking down."

"Someone would've stopped it! They wouldn't let this happen," Ann snapped, crossing her arms.

"An EMP's the perfect weapon," Bonnie insisted. "It doesn't destroy cities—it makes us destroy ourselves."

I watched Bonnie stand her ground. *She's a smart girl, so she'll be a good addition.*

Joe changed the subject. "The deputies are almost done cleaning the weapons we recovered. They'll be back soon to help Clarence and his family unload. Russell and Matthew brought extra gear and ammo that'll help our group."

"I want to join the security team," Bonnie said, her voice firm.

"Let's talk about that later," I said cautiously.

I watched Ann shake a finger at Bonnie. "Over my dead body," she said, her voice loud.

Bonnie flinched. I exchanged a glance with her and gave her a subtle wink. She smiled faintly in return.

Chef C stepped in. "We'll talk it over, Ann. Everyone needs to contribute. Bonnie's already a better shot than most grown men."

"She is not going to be Lara Croft out here!" Ann snapped. "She could get hurt—or killed!"

I chose to stay out of that argument.

"I'm heading to John and Shelly's place tomorrow," I said, changing the subject. "They've got supplies we need to bring back here. We could be gone up to two days. We'll have deputies on security here, and I'll set up the ham radio for communication."

Mel stepped over to Clarence. "Chef. Can I count on you to take the lead on our dietary needs?" she asked. "You know how important it is to ensure we eat right, fuel our bodies to remain strong and healthy. You'll have help, but the kitchen's yours to run. It's a commercial setup in the bunkhouse."

Clarence smiled. "I'll take the role—and I think I've made a new friend here." He looked down at Ruffus, who was still sitting loyally at his feet, tail wagging like he'd found his new best friend.

Chapter 17

Tollbooth to Hell

Once I had Chef C and his family situated, I turned to John. "Let's get the truck and trailer ready for the trip to your place tomorrow. I've got extra gas in cans and siphon gear if we run dry. I figure we leave before dawn, running dark with NVGs."

"Agreed," John replied. "If we leave around zero four hundred, we might clear the hill before daylight hits—assuming no trouble."

"Let's get a meal in us, inspect our gear, and then crash early," I said.

That night, the house smelled of garlic and tomatoes. Mel and Shelly made lasagna for everyone—two trays packed with meat and cheese—served with a green salad fresh from the garden and greenhouse.

"Mel and Shelly. Fabulous dinner. You outdid yourselves. Thank you. Sit down and relax, John and I can help clean up," I said, rubbing my belly.

I started grabbing plates from the table, and the kids joined in.

"Thank you, kids, for helping clean up. Much appreciation," I said as I tousled Charlie and Brian's hair after I placed the last plate in the cupboard.

"Well, kids," I said, with a grin, standing and stretching, my fingers digging into the small of my back. "Time for me to take this fine lady upstairs. Some of us have an early day tomorrow." I wrapped my arm around Mel's waist, and she winked as we disappeared up the stairs.

The alarm went off at zero three hundred. Ruffus gave me the side eye as I slid out of bed. He didn't even try to hide his irritation. When Mel stirred and followed me, he sighed dramatically, slid off the bed, and padded out after her.

While I prepared for the day ahead, Mel was in the kitchen, firing up the stove. The smell of hash browns, eggs, and bacon pulled me downstairs. Ruffus pushed at the door with his nose, making enough space for him to squeeze through. Then, he sat at attention in front of Mel, like a furry beggar.

"Hey mutt. You have a doggy door. Don't be so needy," I said, pointing at Ruffus.

He didn't even look at me, though he heard me as he tucked his ears back while continuing to stare at Mel.

He'd chomped down a couple of bacon strips before Mel cut him off. "That's it. Go lie down."

Ruffus chuffed in protest, circled twice on the couch, and flopped down—eyes locked on her like a betrayed prince.

"You upset the dog," I said.

Mel glanced at Rufus before flipping the bacon. "He gets pushy when food's involved."

I was just about to sit down to eat when John and Shelly showed up. We grabbed a couple of extra plates, and they joined us at the table. "Thank you, sweetheart, for this fine breakfast," I said, and we headed for the shop to gear up.

We grabbed our helmets with NVGs, vests with plates, and extra ammo magazines and weapons. We completed the comms checks, giving each other a thumbs up to confirm we were ready. After outfitting ourselves, I hugged Mel and gave her some parting instructions.

"You know what to do if people show up here unannounced. You have Joe next door, and the deputies. You're trained as well as some of them, though, and listen to their instructions. I'll see you soon, and love you," I said as I released her from a hug.

"I got this," she said. "Be safe, and don't do anything stupid."

"Who, us, do something stupid?" I asked as I got comfortable in the truck.

I climbed into the back seat, and we rolled out in Shelly's truck, trailer in tow, heading down the driveway to the main road. Stopping at the gate, I jumped out to open it and then rearmed it after Shelly had pulled through. We merged onto Highway 88 under the cover of early-morning blackness, heading to their place.

"How long do you think it will take us to get over the hill to your place?" I asked.

"You know, we can usually get there in about two hours, depending on traffic. With the country in the hurt we are now, I suspect five plus hours, and that is if we don't have any issues along the way," John said, in a low voice.

"I agree, and knock on wood, that we have no issues," I replied as I reached up and tapped John on his helmet. He flipped me off, with a smirk.

Running dark, we had NVGs clipped onto our ballistic helmets. These were good for mounting optics and offered protection from small arms.

Looking around, the world was eerily still. We passed Alpine Village without incident, but as we rounded the bend near Kit Carson Campground, my sight flared white through the NVGs. A fire burned on the road. A roadblock.

"Shit," Shelly muttered. "Looks like we've got trouble."

"Get us stopped," I ordered. "I'll dismount, get into the tree line, and set up overwatch. Keep radios on hot mic. If it goes south, I'll lay down cover fire while you two make your move."

John gave a tight nod. "Copy that."

Shelly eased the truck to a crawl, stopping about a hundred yards out. I popped the back door—no interior light to give me away—and slipped into the woods. I scanned the area, searching for something I could use as support. I found a log that I could kneel behind, my weapon balanced on it as I sighted the roadblock ahead.

I whispered into the mic. "Four at the roadblock. One out front and three behind the vehicles—can't tell if anyone else is hidden."

John clicked once in acknowledgment.

A large man—six foot five at least, gut straining against a stretched-out belt—approached the truck. He cradled his rifle lazily across his stomach. Amateur.

Through my headset, I heard John whisper, "Stay calm, sweetheart. Follow my lead."

I watched as the man leaned in through Shelly's window. "What're you doing on the road this early? And without headlights?" He looked around the inside of the truck. "NVGs, huh? Step out of the vehicle so we can inspect it—and you," he added with a lewd laugh. I clenched my jaw, finger finding the trigger guard, and releasing the safety.

"We're headed to Jackson," Shelly replied, her voice calm. "We've got animals to tend. What gives you the right to block the road?"

"Because I've got the gun," Chubby snapped. "This here's my checkpoint. You want through, you pay the toll."

"And if we don't?" John asked, his tone flat.

Chubby chuckled. "Then I'll take what I want—including her." He pointed at Shelly. "She'd do nicely in my harem."

John clicked his tongue three times over the radio. That was the signal.

I prepped my shot. Sights centered on Chubby's chest, I exhaled halfway and squeezed the trigger. The recoil rolled back into my shoulder. A second shot followed immediately, hitting center mass. Chubby dropped like a sack of meat.

John and Shelly were out of the truck immediately, weapons up. The remaining thugs behind the blockade froze. Then I watched as one got brave.

Bad move, buddy.

He popped up just long enough for me to put a 5.56 round through his forehead. The back of his skull blew out in a mist of red and bone as he crumpled behind the vehicle.

John and Shelly advanced, yelling commands. The final two dropped their weapons and raised their hands.

"Clear," John said over the radio.

I moved in.

The two survivors looked barely twenty, trembling and wide-eyed.

"What was the point of this roadblock?" Shelly asked sharply.

The taller one answered. "We were told to take weapons, food … and women. Jeff said he was forming a militia to control the area. He wanted to be the supreme commander," the taller one said, while pointing at the dead guy out front.

"How did that work out?" John asked.

"Not very good," he said, hanging his head.

"They thought they were gonna be warlords or something,"

the kid muttered. "Said they'd protect us if we followed orders."

"Look where that got them," I said in a low rumble. "How many others have you shaken down?"

"You're the second. First group was on foot—had nothing."

"Which way were they headed?" I asked.

"Up the mountain," the kid said, while pointing up the road.

Shaking my head, I said, "Help us move these vehicles. And take the bodies off the road unless you want coyotes all over them. If we pass back through and see another roadblock, we won't be so friendly."

We pushed the cars out of the way, cleared the road, and returned to Shelly's truck. As we pulled away, I looked back at the two kids dragging Chubby's bulk off the pavement. "Let that be a lesson," I muttered. "This new world doesn't have room for self-appointed kings."

Chapter 18

No Easy Road

I saw the early morning rays of sunlight cresting over the ridgeline, chasing the darkness away into the early gray black. I loved watching the sun rise, a painting in motion as it emerged into the early morning sky. The transition of black to deep red and molten gold as the sun clawed for the zenith of the day. I pulled my NVGs up, effectively turning them off as we had enough daylight to see clearly now.

"Let's hope we make the rest of the trip without any more issues," John muttered, his voice low. I was daydreaming as we cruised along the roadway. The hum of the tires on the road making me sleepy. Shelly suddenly slammed on the brakes, making me lurch forward in my seat and become fully awake. A crowd had taken over the pavement. Camped dead center on the road.

I counted about thirty people. "There are too many to drive through, and no time for me to dismount or take up overwatch." My heartbeat ticked upward. "I don't see any weapons," I said, trying to slow my breathing. "But there could be more hiding behind them."

"Same. I'm not liking this one bit," John replied, his jaw clenched. "Why can't we ever just have a damn peaceful drive?"

"Because it's not Sunday, John," I said with a half-grin, trying to cut the tension. "Shelly, keep the truck running. If shooting starts, we'll hit the bed, and you drive."

She stopped thirty feet short of the crowd. John and I stepped out slowly, rifles low but ready.

Their leader approached—a tall, wiry guy in a sweat-stained

Cal Poly pullover, brown 5.11s, and a Dodgers cap so salt-streaked it looked bleached. He raised a hand. "We don't want any trouble," he said, his voice shaking slightly.

"We won't give you any if you don't give us any," I replied. "What's going on here?"

He exhaled sharply. "Most of us were hiking the Pacific Crest Trail when … well, whatever happened, happened. Phones died. None of the cars left in the lot will start. Some of us are running out of food."

I gestured to the group. "How many of you?"

"Forty-five."

John looked at me. "I think we can haul some in the trailer and truck bed—drop them in Jackson."

I nodded. "Alright. We can't take everyone, but we'll get some of you off the mountain. Those in decent shape will need to walk. Jackson's about sixty miles."

"Three to four days for strong hikers," John said as he looked over the group.

"We'll let the authorities know when we get there," I said, though we all knew the odds of a response were low.

The hiker nodded. "I appreciate it."

"You figure out who's riding and who's hiking. No arguments. Anyone who starts a fight stays behind. It'll be a rough ride, but it's better than nothing. If you're riding, consider leaving food behind for the walkers."

He turned to deliver the news. When he returned, I asked him, "What's your name?"

"Tom," he replied. "Somebody had to take charge. People were acting like this was still a weekend trip."

Twenty-five people crammed into the trailer, with an additional five in the truck bed. Tom stayed behind with the remaining fifteen and pointed east. "We're headed toward Minden—it's closer."

"Be safe," I said, climbing back into the cab.

82

Chapter 19

Homecoming

Two hours later, we reached Jackson. Dead vehicles clogged the road, and we had to push several out of the way.

We pulled up to the Amador County Building Department and dropped off our passengers. A young woman, her red hair tucked beneath a dusty pink cap studded with rhinestones that spelled Pink, stepped forward.

"What do we do now?" she asked. "For food or shelter?"

I looked at her, she was geared like a serious hiker—Hollister shirt, 5.11 pants, a full pack with a tent and bedroll.

"Sorry, ma'am," I said with a sigh. "We don't have extra to give. Try the hospital or the sheriff's office; maybe they can help. But we've got nothing for you. Sheriff's office is right there, and the hospital is a block over that way," I said, pointing towards each.

She let out a sigh and turned to the others. "You heard them. No handouts. Let's hope someone in town has a plan."

Leaving the passengers behind, we turned onto Mission Boulevard, then Clinton Road—John and Shelly's place. I grinned. "Ahh … never mind," I said.

"We almost didn't buy the house because of the name on the road," Shelly said, and furrowed her brow. "But it had everything— basement, land, three-car garage, shop. Worth the trade-off."

As we got closer, John grew tense, fidgeting with his rifle. Shelly's grip on the wheel was white knuckled.

"Come in slow," John said. "People know what we do. Our

house is a target."

Shelly eased up the drive. No visible damage. No busted locks or doors.

"Looks untouched," I whispered, not sure why I had lowered my voice.

"Let's clear it," John said. "Then we'll start packing."

John unlocked the door, and I cleared left while he went right. I cleared the four rooms downstairs while John worked the upstairs rooms, checking for signs of entry, but there were no boot prints and no broken windows. Ten minutes later, we stepped back onto the porch.

"All clear," John called.

Shelly met us with a nod. "What's first?"

"You handle clothes. We'll work on food, weapons, and gear," John replied.

We filled totes, buckets, and boxes with food, gear, and prepping supplies. Taking a break, we ate the sandwiches we'd packed from the ranch.

"You think it'll all fit?" I asked, eyeing the trailer—half full already.

"We've got room," John replied. "Still have the bed of the truck."

"And all that ammo," I muttered. "Not looking forward to carrying that."

But we did. 9mm, 5.56, .308, .30-06—all came up. Rarer calibers we locked in the basement armory.

When the last can clanged into the truck bed, I dropped onto the porch steps. "That's everything?" I asked, shaking my arms out after carrying up all the ammo cans. All one hundred and twenty of them.

"That's everything," John said, wiping sweat from his brow.

"I might sleep on the ride back," he smirked.

"Not a chance," Shelly snapped. "You'll be watching for trouble the whole way. This truck's heavy now—acceleration and braking are garbage."

"How's the fuel?"

"Just under three-quarters. We're good."

"Famous last words," I said.

We rolled out slowly, the truck sluggish underneath us. I turned around to look at their house as we left it behind, maybe for the last time.

Chapter 20

The Long Road Home

We retraced our route from John and Shelly's house back through Jackson. When we reached the Amador County Building Department, I noticed about ten of the thirty people we'd dropped off earlier were still there, camped along the edge of the parking lot.

"Shelly, can you pull over for a minute?" I asked.

She stopped the truck, and I climbed out. The group stirred, approaching hesitantly, as if they weren't sure if I was friend or foe. I opened the rear door and hauled out two five-gallon buckets of food.

"This is for you all," I said, setting them down gently. "If you ration this properly, it should last two weeks. Share it wisely. If the hospital or sheriff's office can't help, your best bet is to find some of the local farmers. Offer to work in exchange for food and a place to sleep."

A few heads nodded slowly. One guy looked like he was about to say something.

"Ah h … Never mind," he said.

I turned and climbed back into the truck. "Home, James," I said.

"That was nice of you to give them food and advice," Shelly said as she glanced at me in the rear-view mirror.

"I hope we get good karma from it, and they didn't give us any problems on the trip here. Thought we could help them at least have something after they left all their food on the mountain for the others," I said and grinned back.

"Let's hope for an easy drive …"

"Let's not jinx it," I said, cutting John off. We were long past the point of tempting fate.

Driving back toward Carson Pass, we approached the pullout near the restrooms by the Pacific Crest Trail. Shelly slowed the truck.

Four people stood there, waving at us, trying to flag us down.

"Should we stop?" she asked.

I shook my head. "Nope. Keep moving, I'm not sharing the backseat."

"Not even for a hot redhead?" John asked, turning to look at me with a smirk.

"I've got a hot redhead at home already."

I watched the four people step toward the road, still waving, but we passed them and began our descent out of the mountains.

As we drove through Hope Valley, John leaned forward, resting his arms on the dashboard. "Remember that Jeep trip we did here a few years ago with the club?"

"That was a great trip—except waking up in a frozen tent," I said, rubbing my arms as I remembered how cold I was in that tent. "You two were snuggled up in your RV like royalty."

"Hey, it was colder than usual, even for late summer," John said.

"Remember the scavenger hunt?" I chuckled. "The organizer marked the trail with orange tape, but someone took it all down during the night. We were wandering around like drunk cats in the woods."

"We did eventually find the tower," John said.

"Kit Carson Campground ahead," Shelly said, snapping us out of the nostalgia.

I straightened up, scanning the road and tree line. The same abandoned vehicles were still there, untouched since we'd moved them. It looked clear.

"Keep going," I said, exhaling.

As we descended the last ridgeline, I reached up and keyed the ham radio mic. "Freedom Ranch, actual, calling Freedom Ranch—do you copy?"

After a brief pause, Mel's voice came through, clear and relieved. "Freedom Ranch here. I hear you loud and clear. Where are you? We were getting worried."

"Just passed Woodfords. About thirty minutes out. We'll come in the back way. Can you open the shop? We'll park there and unload tomorrow."

"Copy that. See you soon."

Shelly turned down the gravel road to the ranch. I saw that the sun had slipped behind the Sierra Nevada ridgeline and was casting long, golden shadows across the land. I felt a knot unwind in my chest. We were home.

We pulled up to the shop, the sound of tires on gravel bringing everyone out to greet us. Pushing my door open, I stepped out of the truck and stretched. Mel came running toward me. I caught her as she leapt into my arms, causing me to take a step backwards to keep my balance.

I grinned. "Hey, I missed you too."

"You stink," she teased, holding me tight.

"Battle musk," I said proudly. "We should bottle it and sell it."

"Would never sell," she said.

Ruffus pushed between us, jealous for attention. "I think someone else wants you," Mel said as she hopped down.

I scratched Ruffus behind his ears and under his chin. He chuffed, his tail a blur of motion, and leaned into my leg like he'd missed me, too.

"We'll unload the trailer in the morning," I called out to the group. "It's been a long day. I'm hungry, tired, and probably smell like roadkill."

The crew chuckled as we all filtered out of the shop. Mel locked up behind us.

"Chef C has dinner waiting," Mel announced. "As soon as he heard your voice on the radio, he started cooking."

I stepped into the bunkhouse and could smell the aroma of something incredible.

"Chef C, you're a damn legend," I said as I walked in, pulling off my tactical vest. "You didn't have to go all out."

"It's nothing, TJ. Figured the heroes needed something hot and hearty after a run like that."

John groaned as he dropped onto the couch. "I second that."

Shelly nodded. "Bless you, Chef C."

My plate was hot, and the food Chef C dished up for me, even hotter. We sat in silence around the table, focusing on our food. *Home never tasted so good.*

Chapter 21

Building the Circle

Joe pulled up outside the bunkhouse, just in time for dinner, with the deputies in tow. Matthew and Russell had brought their families to the ranch. As introductions were made, I took in the group: Matthew, his wife Jolene, and their two kids, Isabella and Blake. I recognized Isabella immediately. A rising young gun in the competitive circuit, she and Bonnie were often neck and neck at the local matches.

"Bonnie!" Isabella shouted.

They ran toward each other, squealing with delight, and hugged.

Scarlett, Russell's wife, looked a little wary as she held their boys, Henry and Noah, close.

"I was a dental hygienist … before the world went to hell," she said, almost apologetically.

"That's perfect," I replied. "We'll want to track down dental equipment in town. Clean teeth, happy tribe."

Chef C poked his head out from the kitchen. "Dinner's almost up. Spaghetti and meatballs with fresh greens from Miss Melanie's garden."

"Chef, you're fantastic," I said, already smelling the herbs wafting through the bunkhouse.

"As soon as we finish eating," I added, "we'll get everyone settled. You've got space to spread out—for now. We're looking for bunk beds to expand capacity. Don't get too cozy."

Joe leaned against the counter. "I've got a line on a few more folks to bring in later this week."

As we sat around the long kitchen tables, Bonnie and Isabella ran up, breathless. "If you get bunk beds," Bonnie panted, "can all the girls share a room? We don't want to sleep with smelly boys."

"We'll see," I replied with a grin. "Once we know the full headcount, we'll set up a team to coordinate sleeping arrangements."

Chef C called out, "Dinner is served!" and the room moved in organized chaos. Everyone grabbed a plate, dished up food, and found seats. I counted heads. Twenty-six now. The number kept growing. How far would we expand?

John stood up as people settled with their plates. "Listen up, folks. As we grow, word will spread. Some people will want to join us, others might want what we have. Not everyone's going to come knocking nicely. Security will be necessary, like it or not. We've got weapons and gear. TJ and I will start training those interested in helping defend the ranch. But first, we settle. Then, we train. Then, we organize."

I stood next. "We'll form a leadership team—people we trust to help make decisions. Life-and-death calls? That'll be on Mel and me. But we expect everyone to contribute. This place works only if we work together."

Chef C raised his hand. "A wood-fired stove would save gas and heat the bunkhouse."

I nodded. "Great idea, we'll add it to the scavenger list—along with more gas grills and propane."

Isabella raised her hand. "How do we still have power and water?"

I smiled. "Solar array and battery backup in the shop. Powers the house, bunkhouse, well, and shop. We've got water tanks and pumps tied to the creek, though we'll need to sanitize it before drinking.

Garden and greenhouse get it raw."

Joe chimed in. "There's a place nearby with an old wood cook stove still inside. Might be worth checking out."

"Let's make it a priority," I agreed. "What about security rotations?"

Russell straightened up. "We're in. Whatever's needed."

"You know of any other deputies you'd vouch for?" I asked.

"Nope," Matthew answered firmly. The others agreed.

Joe grinned. "I've got three former Marines at the VFW. They're sharp, loyal, and tough as hell."

"Looking for more crayon eaters, huh?" I teased, getting a few chuckles. "As long as they can pull their weight and not just sit around telling war stories."

Joe rolled his eyes. "They're younger than you. Desert Storm and Afghanistan vets. Good guys. They'd be an asset."

Claire and Tracy perked up. "How old are they?"

"Late twenties," Joe replied with a grin. "Settle down, ladies. No hanky-panky."

I turned toward the door. "Long day. I'm calling it. Mel. You ready to call it a day?" Ruffus was already waiting at the door, tail wagging. "Night, everyone," I said. I walked out into the cool air with Mel just behind me. Ruffus stopped by his usual tree, sniffed the base, then lifted his leg.

"Mail call?" Mel asked, grinning.

"He's gotta check his messages."

Walking up onto the porch, I noticed that John and Shelly were following behind.

"Long day?" I asked.

"Long enough," John muttered.

"Tea before bed?" Mel offered.

"Yes," we all replied in unison.

"It's a new blend—herbal, no caffeine. I'm calling it *Snickerdoodle.*"

We filed into the kitchen, and Ruffus flopped at the base of the stairs, content. The soft glow of lights and the familiar scent of Mel's herbs wrapped around us like a blanket.

For a moment, things felt … normal.

And in a world flipped upside down, that was a rare and beautiful thing.

Chapter 22

Ruffus and the Shadow

The wind had stilled, and that heavy kind of quiet pressed against my eardrums, settling over Freedom Ranch. It was one of those nights when I could feel something was off, even if I couldn't name it. After everything I'd seen in town, I should have been bone tired. But sleep wouldn't come. Instead, I paced the length of the porch, sipping lukewarm coffee from a dented enamel mug.

Ruffus dozed under the porch light, one ear twitching now and then as he tracked the sounds of night creatures. But then he stood up. Not slowly. Not with a stretch and a yawn like usual. He snapped to attention. Nose high. Ears forward. His entire posture shifted in an instant—from lazy companion to coiled protector.

I watched him step off the porch, his paws silent against the gravel, and begin pacing. He moved with purpose, back and forth, then toward the treeline beyond the greenhouse.

I narrowed my eyes as I watched him pace. "You smell something, boy?"

Ruffus stopped. His ears twitched once more, then flattened. Without another sound, he bolted.

I grabbed my rifle and flashlight. "Damn it." I took off after him, the dry leaves and gravel crunching under my boots. The night swallowed sound the deeper I went. The flashlight beam jittered across trees and brush, but the air felt heavier here. Denser. Wrong.

I found him in a clearing we used for morning training drills. He stood stone-still in the center, hackles raised, tail rigid. He wasn't barking. Just a low, constant growl.

Then I saw a shimmer directly in front of where Ruffus had stopped.

I tilted my head, trying to understand what I was seeing. It wasn't a creature, not exactly. Not flesh and blood. The shape was tall—taller than any man—and disturbingly thin. It moved like smoke underwater, flickering at the edges. I couldn't look at it directly. When I tried, my eyes watered, and it blurred out of focus. But when I looked just past it, the outline became clearer. Like heat waves rising off asphalt, but colder. Wrong.

I raised my rifle and flipped the flashlight on. The beam landed on the thing and immediately began to flicker. Then die. The light dimmed until only a dull orange glow remained. My rifle felt heavier in my hands, like gravity itself didn't want me to raise it.

Ruffus barked.

It wasn't a warning. It was a challenge.

The sound broke the spell. The creature hissed—a sharp, metallic sound that made my teeth hurt. It recoiled, folding in on itself, and with a sudden ripple of air, it vanished.

The forest around me snapped back to normal.

Crickets resumed. The wind stirred the leaves again. The flashlight flickered back to full power.

I was breathing hard, my pulse pounding in my ears.

Then I heard it.

Not in the air. Not in the trees.

Inside my head.

He remembers us.

Ruffus walked to my side and pressed his head against my thigh. I looked down at him. His eyes were faintly glowing, not reflected light. A dull, natural luminescence.

"What the hell was that, boy?" I whispered.

He didn't answer, of course. But he stayed close, as if guarding me not just from danger, but from knowledge itself.

I stood there a while longer, staring into the darkness.

Something ancient had brushed against us.

And it remembered.

I wasn't telling Mel anything about this chance encounter, if that's what it was. She already thought I was crazy, all joking aside.

I bolted upright in bed, shivering as chills ran down my body, despite being covered with blankets.

Chapter 23

Roots Beneath

Mel

The early light hadn't yet crested the hills, but in the dream, the glass panels were already aglow with a faint, golden haze. Condensation streaked the inside like breath on a mirror. And the silence … it wasn't ordinary. It pressed against my skin, the kind that comes when the world holds its breath.

I stood barefoot on the packed dirt path between planter boxes, arms crossed, eyes closed. I wasn't tending anything. I wasn't harvesting.

I was listening.

My fingertips brushed the edge of the tomato bed. The soil was cool and damp beneath my hands, dense with the scent of fresh compost and last night's watering. I dropped to my knees and dug my fingers in deeper, palms cradling the earth.

That's when I felt it.

A hum. Faint. Subtle. Like a cello string plucked too gently to hear, but strong enough to feel in the bones. Not from the greenhouse. Not from the wind—there was no wind here.

It came from below.

I opened my eyes.

Light filtered strangely through the glass, thicker than it should've been. Dust motes hung suspended in the air like glitter caught in syrup. Slowly, pressing my hand flat into the dirt, I let the soil cradle my skin.

The hum deepened.

It wasn't sound anymore. It was a sensation. Memory. Recognition.

The tomato vines shifted.

Not from breeze or movement. They moved with purpose. One vine curled toward my wrist and brushed against my skin.

A jolt ran through me, sharp as static but warm like breath.

I gasped and fell backward onto my hands.

The greenhouse remained still.

But where my hand had been, the soil bulged slightly, threadlike roots pressing upward in a circular pattern. Not random. A spiral. Intentional.

I backed away. Not in fear. Not exactly.

But something inside me whispered, *You were not supposed to see this yet.*

I looked at the rows of spinach, carrots, and herbs. Everything seemed … sharper. Brighter. Listening back.

I wiped my hands on my jeans, but there was no dirt. My palms glowed faintly—just for a moment—before returning to normal.

A memory flickered.

A forgotten dream within the dream: roots curling around my legs, pulling me into the earth as whispers echoed in a language I didn't understand, but felt like home.

I hadn't told anyone.

Not even TJ.

I stood and walked toward the greenhouse door. As I opened it, a warm wind stirred behind me, rustling the leaves with a sound like a sigh.

I woke with a start.

Sunlight was breaking across the ranch. The sheets were tangled around my legs. Ruffus lay at the foot of the bed, one eye open, watching.

I sat up slowly, rubbing my eyes.

Even though it had only been a dream, I could still feel the dirt on my hands.

That felt so real.

Ruffus crawled up next to me to cuddle.

"What up, boy? Did you feel me rustling the covers?" I asked

He gave me a little chuff as I scratched the top of his head, and he nosed my cheek as if saying, "I know what you felt, Mama."

Chapter 24

Dawn Patrol

TJ

The morning came early, as usual. No matter how hard I tried to sleep in, I couldn't. My brain was already ticking, and my body knew it. I could feel Ruffus lying between Mel and me. He must have crawled up to my pillow at some point and lay his big head down next to Mel's, content to snuggle until she stirred.

I headed downstairs, the taste of toothpaste lingering on my tongue. Ruffus followed shortly. He made a beeline for the door, looked at me, then looked back. "Silly dog. You have your own door," I said, but I opened the door and left it ajar anyway so he could patrol the perimeter.

He didn't even look at me as he headed outside.

The air was cold as I stepped into the kitchen. I placed the old-fashioned percolator on the stove. The bubbling promise and rich aroma of caffeine filled the room. My brain had wanted that boost ten minutes ago.

Ruffus returned, his nails clicking on the floor as he padded toward me. I scratched his head; he nudged my hand with approval, tail thumping. A second later, he perked up, ears like twin radar dishes, scanned the air.

John came around the corner just as the coffee finished.

"How did you know it'd be ready?" I asked.

"I heard you come down. We make ours the same way at

home."

"Old habits die hard," I said, handing him a cup.

We stepped out onto the porch, coffee in hand, and watched the sun crest the horizon. Ruffus wandered back upstairs—probably to snuggle Mel again.

"Coffee just tastes better out here," John said, taking a sip. "This view … this air … it's damn near perfect."

"One of the reasons we bought this place. East-facing porch, always a front-row seat to a new day."

John's face turned thoughtful. "You've read every prepper book out there, TJ. What do you really think is coming for us?"

I exhaled slowly. "Wish I had a crystal ball. My gut says most won't make it—disease, starvation, violence. We saw what happened on the way home from Rubicon. People lost their damn minds as soon as they realized no help was coming. We're better off than most, but it's going to get ugly."

"Does any of that scare you?" he asked.

"All of it."

He nodded. "This place is a lifeline. Let's keep working together."

Before I could reply, I heard Ruffus's claws again.

"I think Mel's up. I hear him on the floor."

"I doubt Shelly's up," John said with a grin. "She loves her sleep."

The door creaked open, and Shelly walked up behind John and smacked him on the back of the head.

"Why would I miss a sunrise like this?" she asked.

"Ouch! I know you love your bea—uh, sleep," he stammered.

"Careful," she growled. "No coffee yet. I'm worse than

hangry."

Mel joined us on the porch, a coffee cup in her hand. We sat and watched as sunlight streaked through scattered clouds, painting the sky in gold and orange.

"What's on the agenda?" Mel asked.

I took one look at the fading sunrise. "Check on the Marines, see about bunk beds, and evaluate our security posture." I raised my cup—only to find it empty. "Any coffee left?"

"Nope. We finished it," Mel said, standing and gathering the cups. "But Chef C might be cooking."

At the mention of food, Ruffus bolted off the porch like a launched missile. He waited for us on the path to the bunkhouse, looking at us, then back at the bunkhouse, his tail wagging.

The scent of bacon hit me halfway down the trail.

I sniffed the air. "I smell bacon!"

Inside, the griddle hissed with bacon and hash browns, and coffee was brewing nearby. Ruffus had found Chef C and was already begging like a pro.

Joe pulled up on his ATV, sending a cloud of dust over the bunkhouse.

"Morning, kids!" he called out. "Great day to be alive."

He wore one of his infamous Cross-Rifle Company shirts. The front read *Lube Up*, and the back had a cartoon AR bolt with the words, *Because Nobody Likes a Dry Bolt*.

Chef C called out, "How do you want your eggs?"

"Over easy, peasy," I replied.

After Ruffus had scoffed a couple of strips of bacon, I warned Chef not to spoil him. Ruffus looked up at me, his ears flicked back, giving me a glare like I had just stood on his tail. After we ate, the kids gathered up the plates, cleaned down the tables and washed the dishes, earning high praise—and first dibs on future meals.

We walked over to the shop to unload John and Shelly's gear. After organizing our trade supplies, our buckets of food, ammo, silver, and gold, we packed up for town.

"Joe, are you driving your truck?" I asked.

"Yeah. I need a partner for security."

"Everyone got vests and plates?" I asked. Joe shook his head.

"To the armory, then."

They followed me into the armory, and jaws dropped. I handed out suppressed AR-15s, though Joe stuck with his M1. I assigned roles once everyone was loaded up. We were almost ready to head out when Tracy ran up.

"Can Claire or I come? If we hit the drugstore, we could help gather supplies."

"Great idea," I said. I got her outfitted with a vest, an AR, a Walther PDP, and magazines.

"I would like to carry the pistol I brought with me," she said, then she admired herself. "I feel like Lara Croft!"

I shook my head. "I like us all to have the same brand and style of weapons. If we get into a firefight, we can share magazines and ammo."

"I get it. Let's roll," she said.

Ruffus chuffed at me when I tapped him on the head and pointed to the back seat. He headed to the back seat, muttering canine protests.

Just past the city limit sign, we saw the roadblock. They were armed and on alert, watching us. I pulled my Jeep to a stop 200 yards back.

Dylan pulled up beside me and leaned out of the window. "We can bypass. There's an alley about fifty feet back."

I put the Jeep into reverse, then swung into the alley. We were nearing the VFW when we heard gunfire. I braked hard and pulled into cover. I dropped my head down to look out the front windscreen and up at the VFW roof. "Someone's attacking the VFW."

Joe joined me. "I know those guys on the roof—local vets."

"I think we can flank these attackers," I said. "John and I will circle around. Joe, wait for our call."

John, Ruffus, and I climbed out of our Jeeps and crouched as we crossed the road, gaining the cover of the building on the other side. We ran through the alley, coming out behind the thugs. I radioed, "TJ and John in position."

"On three … One. Two. Three. Fire."

My first shot went through the side of his head and out the other, blood and bone spraying over the pavement. I shifted my aim to the second thug, centered my sights on his head, and pulling the trigger, I saw the result of the bullet impacting his head. More blood and bone material, spraying across the pavement. I could hear John double-tap another. Joe's M1 roared, and a fourth dropped with a devastating exit wound. The VFW crew joined in, their shots ringing out. The final assailants were cleared in a matter of moments.

"Joe, get up here," I called. "These guys trust you more."

Joe walked out in front of us. "Hey! It's Joe. Don't shoot!"

A voice replied, "I recognize your old truck, leatherneck."

We met at the entrance. Joe introduced me to Nick, Carlos, and Gavin—former Marines who'd settled locally post-service.

"You're John Packard of JP Tactical, aren't you?" Carlos asked.

"Guilty."

"We meant to take your course."

"Well," I grinned, "it's free now if you want to join us at the ranch," I replied.

I watched them all nod their heads in agreement. Gavin seemed to take an interest in Tracy, not taking his eyes off her.

Joe pointed at the truck. "Leathernecks, load your asses into the truck, and let's get your gear and you out to TJ's ranch."

I nudged Tracy away from her new crush. "You can make googly eyes later. Focus up."

"Did not," she protested.

"Did too," I teased, walking back with her to the Jeep.

Mel's voice crackled over the radio. "Crowd forming at the main gate. Might be trouble. We're taking defensive positions."

"We're on our way," I replied.

Ruffus shifted in the back, his ears perked, and his body tense.

Another day in paradise.

Chapter 25

Trouble at the Gate

Mel

Waiting for TJ's call to bring more trade goods to the furniture store, Melissa burst into the bunkhouse, out of breath and wide-eyed.

"There's a group of people at the gate!" she exclaimed. "They're trying to climb over, but they can't get through."

"Grab the guys and the weapons. Head for the gate. I'll call TJ," I ordered, looking around for my radio.

I closed my eyes. "Damn it. I've left the radio on the kitchen counter." I scanned the room. "Who else has a radio?"

Russell walked in, his brows furrowed. "What's going on? Melissa just sprinted past me."

"There's a crowd at the front gate," I said. "Let me use your radio—I need to alert TJ now."

"Here," he said, handing it over. "I'll grab the rest of the team, and we'll move into position."

"Thank you," I said, taking the radio.

I raised the radio and hit the transmit button. "TJ, it's Mel. We've got a situation, people are at the front gate trying to get in."

Static buzzed for a half-second before TJ's voice cut through, tense but calm. "On our way."

I knew he wouldn't waste a second. If anything, he was already flooring it.

I jogged toward the road leading to the gate, passing Russell and the others moving with purpose, weapons in hand, scanning the tree line as they advanced. They weren't just my friends or neighbors anymore; we were a unit, and I could see them falling into formation like professionals.

I reached the gate and saw what Melissa had described: a group of maybe fifteen or twenty people scattered along the fence line, some yelling, some pacing, a few trying to scale it without success. They looked ragged, desperate. Too desperate.

I found a position that allowed me to monitor the crowd and assess the situation without being exposed. Russell plopped down next to me, breathing heavily. "What do you think we should do?" I asked.

"We need to give our team a few minutes to get into final positions, and while they are doing that, we can monitor the group and look for weapons or other threats," he replied through heavy breaths.

I was about to say something about him needing more cardio when I heard the racing of the engine in TJ's Jeep coming down the road. I heard the tires skidding across the pavement as he slammed on the brakes, and then they bit for traction. He was coming in hot.

I exhaled, tension curling in my gut. Whatever this was, it was about to come to a head.

Chapter 26

Standoff at the Gate

TJ

We had enough people at the ranch to mount a solid defense if needed, but having more skilled individuals would have been even better. I grabbed the radio and keyed up. "Joe, if you and your Marine buddies want to join us at the gate, that'd be great. If this goes hot, I'd rather have extra firepower in trusted hands."

"Copy that," Joe replied. "Two minutes behind you."

I clicked my radio microphone button. "We're taking the same route back—remember the roadblock we detoured around? Be prepared. Weapons free if fired upon. Joe, swing around and approach from your side of the property. If this turns into a pincer movement, so be it."

"Copy. Rolling now," Joe confirmed.

We passed the town limits. The roadblock was still there, manned and waiting. I slammed my foot down and pushed the Jeep harder. Ruffus leaned forward, his body tense. I could tell he could sense the shift in mood.

"You ready, buddy?"

He chuffed in reply.

The gate came into view, and I stomped on the brakes. The tires squealed in protest, BFG tires leaving long black lines on the pavement. John pulled up beside me in Shelly's truck, his crew jumping out to form a defensive line.

Ruffus vaulted from the Jeep. Tracy followed and flanked me while the others took position.

About twenty people stood outside the gate, disorganized but lingering. Some paced. A few looked around nervously. I couldn't see any visible weapons—yet.

"Anyone see guns?" I asked over the radio.

"Negative," came the replies.

"Stay sharp," I replied. "I'm stepping out."

I moved from behind the door and shouted, "What do you want at my gate?"

A man stepped forward—tall, mid-fifties, clean-shaven, wearing a damn suit of all things.

"That's far enough!" I barked when he got within twenty feet.

"We need food and shelter," he said. "Heard there was a ranch run by preppers out this way. The town's gone sideways. Gangs are taking over."

He inched forward. Ruffus snapped out a sharp bark.

"Control your dog," the man snapped.

I smirked. "He's here to protect me, not you. And you're still outside my gate."

Joe came over the radio. "We're fifty feet behind the group on the other side. Ready if this turns south."

I clicked twice in acknowledgment.

"I'm not accepting guests," I said firmly. "Though if I were, why should I let you in?"

"I'm the manager of the local bank," he replied. "I can help manage things here."

"A bank manager?" I raised a brow. "So, you don't do hard labor. You like telling people what to do?"

"That's what a manager does," he said without shame and a smirk on his lips.

"What do you do for fun?" I asked, knowing the answer would seal it.

"Golf and travel," he said with a small, proud smile.

"Right. You can't dig, can't shoot, can't hunt. How about the others? Anyone got useful skills?"

"I … I don't know. We didn't have time to talk. We just left."

"Look," I said, my voice sharp, "this isn't a charity. We're running a survival operation, not a cruise ship. No food, no shelter, no camping near the gate. You all need to move along."

He stiffened. "So, that's it? You're turning your back on people in need?"

"You need skills and the will to contribute. Do you even know how to skin a deer? Grow a tomato? This is hard living. If you can't work, you're a liability. And if anyone tries to come over this fence," I raised my voice, "we will shoot."

The man turned back to the group and addressed them. "They're not letting us in. They're armed, and they won't hesitate. We need to go." Most of them turned, heading reluctantly in the direction Joe was watching. But two figures lingered—one woman and a young girl.

"Sir," the woman said, watching me cautiously. "May I speak with you?"

I nodded, motioning her forward slightly.

She was tall and blonde with an athletic build. Her daughter, about fifteen, wore pink flip-flops and a light blue CRCC shirt.

"I was the town vet," she said. "I can help with livestock, pets, even people in a pinch. I've patched up worse than a few ranch wounds."

"Wait here," I said, and turned, waving over John. I grabbed my radio. "Mel, meet me at the gate." Mel arrived a few moments later. "She's a vet, thinks she can help."

Mel's hand shot out, aiming for the back of my head. I ducked. "Let her in, you idiot. That's a vital skill," she scolded.

"On it," I muttered and turned back.

I approached the woman and her daughter again. "My wife and I talked. We'd like to offer you a place. What are your names?"

"Gail, and this is my daughter, Katie."

"You'll be expected to work, pull your weight, and not be a jerk. No blood rituals or weird chants required."

Katie grinned. "Kind of like *Grumpy Old Men* out here."

John and I both glared, but Ruffus made the final judgment. He sniffed Katie's hand and licked it. She giggled and reached to scratch behind his ears. He leaned into it, his tail thumping.

"Looks like Ruffus approves," I said.

Gail scratched him, too, and he sat beside her like an old friend.

"Do you have a husband we need to go look for?" I asked gently.

Her face fell. Katie answered for her. "Dad died in Afghanistan. It's just been us." Ruffus leaned in again and licked Gail's hand as a tear slid down her cheek.

"I'm so sorry," I said softly. "Welcome to Freedom Ranch. We've got a couple of trauma nurses already. You'll fit right in. We'll set up a clinic together."

Mel opened the gate and hugged both Gail and Katie as they stepped in. "Come on. I'll get you settled," she said.

The rest of us loaded into vehicles and rolled back toward the bunkhouse. The smell of Chef C's cooking hit us before we stepped through the door.

I turned to Chef C, unable to hide my anticipation. "Chef, what's for lunch?" I asked, practically drooling at the thought of a hot meal. "Grilled cheese with tomato-basil soup."

A chorus of "Yesss!" followed.

Mel ushered Gail and Katie to the front of the line.

After lunch, I pulled Gail aside. "Do you need anything from town? Clothes, gear, supplies?"

"Yes," she said. "We've got stuff in the house that would help us live better out here."

"Perfect. We're heading back to find that furniture store owner anyway. We'll swing by and grab your things."

I looked across the room. Tracy and Gavin were talking quietly, sitting way too close. I made a note of it.

"Nick, Carlos," I called. "We got cut short earlier. We'll take you back to your place while the rest of us check out the furniture store. Then we'll pack up Gail's place."

"Sounds like a plan, Stan," Nick said with a grin.

We jumped into our trucks and headed out again. I sent Gail with Joe and Dylan. "Katie can stay if you want," I offered.

"I want to play with the other kids," she said with excitement.

"Okay, but behave and listen to Miss Mel," Gail warned.

"Yes, Mom," she said, running off to join the others.

Chapter 27

Glimmers in the Ashes

Mel

I stretched my hands over my head. It had been a long but productive day. New patrol schedules had been posted. TJ, John, and the rest of the crew had headed back out toward town to track down bunk beds and supplies. I took a breather with the rest of the crew as the afternoon sun cast warm shadows over Freedom Ranch. I sat near the garden plots and watched the kids and Ruffus chase each other like it was still a normal summer day.

It wasn't, of course. The world had changed.

I looked around at the people we had gathered—deputies, veterans, nurses, cooks, and even a few wandering souls trying to rebuild their lives. What we had here wasn't just a community. It was becoming something more … something purposeful. I wasn't sure if we were building a safe haven or training for a war. Maybe both.

Shelly sat beside me on one of the rough-cut benches by the greenhouse, her water bottle balanced between her knees. We sat in companionable silence for a moment, and I watched the wind play across the tall grass.

Then I turned to her. "Have you had any … unusual dreams since the EMP?"

She looked over, one brow arched. "Unusual? You mean aside from the usual apocalyptic nightmares and random trauma flashes?"

I shook my head. "No. I mean, it's strange. Surreal. Almost

… magical."

Shelly's expression changed—subtle, but noticeable. She leaned forward. "Yeah. Yeah, I have. Crystals. Big ones. Glowing like they were alive. Sometimes I'm throwing them, and sometimes they just float around me. One was so big I could ride it. Like I was flying over a shattered world."

I felt my breath hitch. "That's … almost exactly what I've seen. My hands glow in mine. I can feel energy pulsing through them like I'm holding lightning. Plants swaying to my voice as I talk to them. It's not just dreams, Shelly. It feels like something's waking up."

She stared out across the fields, thoughtful. "I've never had dreams like that before. Not even during the most stressful deployments, when TJ was gone. I usually remember my dreams—but these … these hit different."

"Do you think it's connected to the EMP?"

"Maybe," she said. "Maybe the EMP wasn't just the death of tech. Maybe it cracked something open. Something old."

We fell silent again, the weight of that thought settling between us. Out here, with the birds chirping and the kids laughing, it didn't feel like the end of the world. But under the surface, something was stirring. Something we hadn't trained for.

Across the courtyard, the deputies lay out an obstacle course. They moved with precision, muscle memory from lives once dedicated to war. But now, they were part of something else. A new world was forming, and every survivor who joined us changed its shape.

"The Marines bring a lot to the table," Shelly said, nudging me with her elbow. "Professionalism. Strategy. And honestly? They're easy on the eyes."

I smirked. "Can't argue with that."

"That's no lie," Claire said, suddenly appearing with perfect timing. She fanned herself with exaggerated flair. "You see Tracy and Gavin by the water barrels? Flirting like teenagers on a field trip."

"Hooks are already being set," Shelly said, laughing. "This new world's going to be strange for dating, that's for sure."

"Strange doesn't even cover it," I murmured.

We were quiet for a beat, watching the kids play in the yard. The kind of normal human moment that had become rare and precious.

"You ever think," I said slowly, "that whatever's happening to us … these dreams, the instincts, even Ruffus acting more aware than a normal dog—that it might be some kind of evolution?"

Shelly shrugged, but I saw her jaw tighten. "Or a curse. Or a calling. Hell, maybe both."

Ruffus trotted past us, paused, and turned to look directly at me, head tilted, ears alert like he'd heard every word. He gave a short huff, then padded off toward the bunkhouse. Claire drifted away to help in the bunkhouse, and Shelly and I sat a little longer, soaking in the light while it lasted. Whatever came next, it wasn't going to be easy, but for the first time in a long while, I didn't feel alone facing it.

I had my people. I had my strange new dreams. And I had a sense—deep in my bones—that something bigger was just beginning.

Chapter 28

The Glimmering Veil

I looked out across Freedom Ranch. The moon hung low, casting silver light across the bunkhouse roof. The evening had settled quietly, save for Ruffus's occasional chuffing sigh near the porch steps and the steady chirp of insects. Inside, most had turned in early—fatigue finally catching up after the tension of the day.

Shelly stood outside the bunkhouse with me, sipping the last of the scotch from a tin cup. The distant ridgeline looked almost ghostlike in the moonlight. A breeze stirred the leaves behind the greenhouse, and for just a second, I thought I saw something glint— like fireflies, but brighter.

Shelly noticed too. "You saw that?" she asked, her voice low. "I did."

We walked slowly toward the garden. The air around the greenhouse felt … different. Heavier. The breeze had vanished, and the silence pressed in like cotton over the ears. I reached for the flashlight clipped to my belt and flicked it on.

The light barely cut through the dark, but then we saw them— crystals. They hovered in the air like weightless shards of glass, softly pulsing with color. One was deep blue, another pulsed greenish gold. They floated, almost beckoning.

"I've seen these," Mel whispered. "In my dreams."

"So have I."

One of the shards drifted closer. It hovered near my hand, as if waiting for permission. I reached toward it—just a few inches—and as soon as my fingertips brushed its surface, the world dropped out from beneath me.

I stood in a burning city.

The sky was black with smoke, and lightning crackled through unnatural clouds. All around me were people—armed, screaming, fighting—but their faces were blurred, their bodies glowing slightly, like heat off pavement.

Ruffus stood beside me, fully transformed into a Gryphon—a being of feathers, fur, and flame. His wings beat once, and the world trembled.

Ahead, on the highest rooftop, stood a woman made of crystal and fire, a crown of light above her head. She looked down at me and said one word.

"Awaken."

I jolted back, gasping. Shelly caught me by the shoulders.

"You okay?" she asked.

"I … yeah. Yeah. What the hell was that?"

"I saw something too," she murmured. "But mine was … the earth. It opened up. Pulled me down into roots, fire, stone. And then I was thrown back out with something glowing in my hand."

We looked down. The shards were gone.

"What did it mean?" I asked.

"I think it means we're changing."

Behind us, Ruffus barked once. I turned. He stood rigid, staring at the tree line. A second later, he growled low and deep. Something moved in the darkness—too tall for a man, too smooth in its gait.

Shelly and I raised our rifles in unison, but Ruffus stepped forward, planting himself between us and the trees. It came again— that pulse, that weight in the air. The figure stopped, looked toward us, then faded back into the brush.

We didn't speak. Just stared. Whatever it was … it wasn't human. Not anymore.

I stood in the kitchen, by the dead Keurig, playing with a coffee pod, unable to sleep.

We'd learned to prepare for many things—EMP, war, collapse. But this … this was something else.

A war was coming.

And it wouldn't just be fought with bullets.

Chapter 29

Barter and Bunkbeds

TJ

We loaded up and rolled out, taking the same detour we'd used to skirt the roadblock of the wannabe warlords near Walmart. Joe broke off from our convoy a few blocks out, heading to Nick's place with Carlos and Gavin to pack up their gear. John and I continued deeper into town, navigating the eerily quiet streets, until we reached the furniture store.

As expected, the storefront was locked up tight, its windows dusty and dim. No signs of movement inside.

"Let's circle around back," I said over the radio. "The owner lives just across the alley. If he's not inside, we'll yell loud enough for him to hear us."

John clicked his mic in acknowledgment.

I killed the Jeep engine after pulling into the narrow alley behind the building. Climbing out, I walked to the rear entrance of the store and knocked sharply on the door. The hollow sound echoed in the alleyway. For a moment, nothing happened, just silence and still air.

Then a figure appeared from the back porch of the neighboring house. A man walked toward us, moving with the kind of stiffness earned from decades of honest labor. He looked familiar, but older than I remembered.

Then a figure emerged from the back porch of the neighboring house. A man stepped toward us—noticeably younger than I remembered, his movements purposeful and alert. His eyes scanned the alley with cautious awareness, as if he was fully attuned to the dangers that might be lurking nearby.

The man approached us, his gaze wary and his tone measured as he spoke. "What can I do for you?" he asked, making it clear that he was not expecting visitors. He glanced at the empty storefront and shook his head. "Store's closed. No power, and the world's gone to shit." His words hung in the air, a blunt acknowledgment of the state of things, and an indication that normal business was no longer possible under current circumstances."Mr. Tinkerton? It's TJ," I said, stepping forward. "We bought beds and a few other things from you a couple of years back for our bunkhouse. I could use more—ten sets of bunk beds, if you have them. They don't have to match. We're trading now. I brought goods."

"I might have that many. Not taking cash, though. Credit cards are worthless now, and I can't run them anyway," he said

"Understood," I said. "I brought five AR-15s, a thousand rounds of ammo, and five buckets of long-term food. Thirty servings per bucket. I've got gold and silver too, if that matters."

He stroked his chin. "Gold and silver might be worth something later, but I can't eat them. Tell you what—keep three of the rifles, double the food, and we'll have a deal."

"Deal," I said without hesitation. "I'll radio the ranch and get the rest sent over."

I stepped back to the Jeep and keyed up. "TJ calling Freedom Ranch. We need five more food buckets sent our way. Use the detour around Walmart—the roadblock's still up."

"Copy," Mel's voice crackled back. "We're loading now."

I turned back to Tinkerton. "If you show us where the beds

are, we'll get started loading. Trade goods are en route."

"Fair enough," he grunted, pulling out a ring of old brass keys. "Back door's this way."

We followed him inside. The scent of cedar and old upholstery filled the cool, dark space. A moment later, the rattle of a chain and the creak of steel echoed through the back as he rolled up the loading dock door. He pointed out a neatly stacked row of bunk bed frames and mattresses.

I moved the trailer closer to the loading dock and began loading bunk beds and mattresses. I had most of them loaded when John pulled into the alley, when Mel came over the radio.

"Where are you guys?"

"Back by the loading dock," I replied.

Mel pulled around and parked. Gail climbed out with her, surveying the space with quiet curiosity. "Where do you want us to put the trade goods?" Mel asked, already popping open the tailgate.

Tinkerton raised a hand. "Let me grab my kids to help carry this. They're still home."

He jogged through his backyard and returned with his two teenagers in tow. The boy, maybe seventeen, nodded once and hoisted two food buckets without a word. The girl, close to sixteen, followed him with another. They worked efficiently. When the last bucket was hauled away, I handed over two ARs and magazines from Mel's gear bag. The boy accepted his new rifle like it was a rite of passage, slinging it over his shoulder with silent pride.

We finished loading the bunk beds and secured them in the trailer.

"Gail," I called over. "We've got extra room in the trailer. Let's hit your place and pack up your things next. But first, let's swing by the VFW and check in with Joe and the guys."

I turned back to Tinkerton. "Thank you for the deal. If you ever need anything, or if your situation changes, you know where to find us."

"I appreciate it," he replied. "We're staying here as long as we can."

As we pulled away, I glanced back to see him watching from his back porch, one hand resting protectively on his daughter's shoulder.

We headed toward the VFW. As we neared the block, I spotted Joe's truck parked outside Nick's house—and the ridiculous mountain of gear they were trying to fit into it. Mattresses leaned awkwardly across the tailgate, and a chair stuck out one window like a tongue wagging at gravity.

I laughed so hard I had to slow the Jeep.

"Looks like you're trying to pack ten pounds of shit into a five-pound bag," I said over the radio.

"Shut up," Joe replied. "We'll make it fit."

"You're going to look like the damn Beverly Hillbillies driving home."

Joe looked at me with his eyes narrowed, lips pursed, and chin tucked. "Bite your tongue, young man. All this stuff is essential."

"Sure it is," I teased. "Let's open the back of the trailer. You can load the overflow so we don't spend all day playing Tetris with your gear. You can leave the mattresses, though."

Once the last of it was loaded—chairs, bedding, ammo cans, a tactical coffee grinder—we headed for Gail's house. There were still miles to go before sunset, but for the first time in days, the tension had lifted. There was work to be done, sure—but it was for something that mattered.

Chapter 30

Unwelcome Attention

I led our convoy further into town with Gail giving directions to her house from the passenger seat. As we pulled up to her street, the view ahead made me uneasy—Walmart was just a few blocks down. And if any of those gang members we'd dodged earlier were still holed up there, this wasn't going to be a quiet stop.

Gail's place was a charming little ranch home, eggshell blue with white shutters and trim. The yard was neat, fenced with chain-link, and dotted with a few wind-blown flower beds. It stood out in the ruined silence of the town; it felt like a memory trying to stay alive.

Once we parked, Gail made a beeline for the front door with Mel close behind. Joe and the Marines spread out immediately, establishing a perimeter without needing to be told. They moved like clockwork—quiet, efficient, alert.

John and I stepped inside to help. "Just pack the essentials—for you and Katie," I told Gail as she moved into the kitchen. "We've got food, water, and supplies back at the ranch."

"I … I don't have enough boxes," she said, her voice catching. "I don't know how I'm going to get it all …"

I placed a hand on her shoulder. "If you've got trash bags in the kitchen, we'll use those. It'll work out."

Mel gave her a hug and followed her down the hallway toward the bedrooms with Shelly. I grabbed the box of garbage bags from under the sink and tossed a few toward John. We worked on taking anything useful from the kitchen.

Ten minutes later, Gail and Mel reappeared with bundles of clothes, toiletries, and a few photo frames.

"This is the last of it," Gail said, her voice still wavering.

"Take a minute," I told her. "Grab whatever little keepsakes you can. Pictures, heirlooms. After this, we roll out. We're too close to trouble for my taste."

I stepped outside with a load for the trailer just as Carlos's voice came in over the radio.

"Heads up," he said, tight and urgent. "We've attracted attention. A group from Walmart is headed this way. Armed."

"I see them," Dylan added a second later. "Red bandanas. White T-shirts, jeans, Vans. Local gang. Dangerous. Trigger-happy."

"Shit," I mumbled.

I snapped the trailer doors shut and looked over as Gavin popped the tailgate on Joe's truck and pulled out a long, black foam-lined rifle case. He flipped it open and revealed a military-grade sniper rifle—complete with a high-magnification optic and five loaded mags.

"Hold this," he said to Nick as he climbed onto the trailer. He went prone, flipped out the bipod, and started scanning.

Carlos's voice came again, sharper. "Taking fire! Falling back! Cover me!"

"Got 'em," Gavin muttered. He fired. The shot cracked like a thunderclap in the narrow street.

I looked just in time to see a gang member drop. Gavin's round had hit center mass, but the sheer power of it shredded the man's upper chest. Blood sprayed across a parked car like red mist. Gavin adjusted and fired again. Another target went down.

John emerged from the house, guiding Gail and Mel behind the trailer for cover. They crouched low, backs to the steel, safe for the moment.

I moved up the side of the street, using abandoned vehicles for cover. I spotted Dylan between two sedans, reloading. "There—fifty feet, left side," I whispered, pointing out two threats sneaking down the sidewalk. I popped up and fired—two controlled shots per target. They both collapsed, dead before they could even register they'd been hit.

Gavin's rifle cracked again. "Threat down."

More bursts of fire from Carlos and Nick echoed across the block. Our side was calm, deliberate. The gang was falling apart fast.

One by one, the gang members dropped or scattered. I watched one of them toss his weapon and sprint down the alley. Gavin didn't even flinch.

"Looks like they've had enough," he called out.

"Status?" I asked over the radio.

"All clear here," came the replies—Nick, Carlos, Dylan.

"Do we sweep for survivors?" Nick asked.

"Negative," I answered. "We're not sticking around long enough for their friends to regroup. Load up. We're out."

Gavin climbed down from the trailer, broke down his rifle, and stowed it. In minutes, we were back in our vehicles, dust kicking up as we left Gail's block behind.

I grabbed the mic. "Freedom Ranch, this is TJ. We're inbound. ETA seven minutes."

"Copy," Matthew replied, his voice steady.

As we sped out of town, the adrenaline still thrumming in my veins, I glanced in the rearview mirror. Gail's house was getting smaller by the second, fading into the distance like so many pieces of the old world. Another line crossed. Another reason to keep moving forward.

As the outskirts of town gave way to open country roads, the tension in my chest finally began to ease. We had the beds, we had Gail's gear, and—by some miracle—we hadn't lost anyone. But this skirmish was a warning shot from the new world we now lived in. The rules had changed. Survival wasn't just about food and firepower anymore. It was about who we trusted, how we adapted, and what we were willing to become. And with each mile closer to Freedom Ranch, that line between who we used to be and who we were becoming grew a little thinner. Ahead, the sun dipped low on the horizon, casting golden light across the road home. Whatever came next, it would start there.

Chapter 31

Signals in the Silence

TJ

We pulled into Freedom Ranch just as the sun was kissing the horizon. I parked the trailer in front of the bunkhouse, and the dust from our journey hadn't even settled before the hugs and high-fives started flying. We'd had a couple of battles, and since we hadn't lost anyone, we weren't mourning a loss or counting wounds—we'd completed our mission and survived a firefight. That was worth celebrating.

"Hey, Nick," I called out, "anything in Joe's truck you want inside the bunkhouse?"

"Just my rifle, if that's alright. I'd like to keep it close."

"That's fine," I replied, nodding. "Let's hope you won't need to use it. We've got a lot of kids running around, though we're planning to give everyone proper training."

I told him the rest of his gear could wait. "We'll store most of it in the armory at the shop. I'll show you guys. There's a large one there and a smaller one in the house."

"How large is 'large'?" Nick asked with a skeptical smirk.

I grinned. "Get ready to be impressed."

We were greeted by pure chaos in the bunkhouse as the last of the bunk beds were unloaded and set up. Nick, Gavin, and Carlos followed me toward the shop, still doubtful. There were new faces, half-unpacked bags, bunk beds needing assembly, and the combined energy of a group learning to breathe as one.

"The shop is a hundred by forty feet," I explained as we walked. "The armory in here is thirty by fifteen. The one in the house has my personal favorites."

Joe snorted from behind them. "Don't let him fool you. His 'small' armory's not that much smaller—and both are loaded."

Nick raised an eyebrow, visibly more interested.

When I unlocked the armory and opened the door, all three of them froze.

"Holy shit," they muttered in unison.

Inside, the room was lined with organized racks of AR-15s, AR-10s, and bolt-action rifles, as well as shelves of neatly stacked ammunition. A wall of pistols was displayed like a showroom. A reloading bench sat at the back, automated equipment gleaming under overhead lights.

"Just a modest selection," I said with a shrug. "Most of these have seen action—none of them are safe queens. I shoot competitively, so everything here has a purpose."

Carlos looked around, eyes wide. "This is insane. I've never seen a private collection like this."

"We'll organize your gear here," I added, pointing to an empty section of the wall. "You'll each get a key. You're free to use anything—but treat it like your own."

Then I opened a drawer and pulled out a box. "And in case you guys get hungry …" I held up a box of crayons.

Carlos nearly doubled over laughing. "We are never leaving this room."

We stacked weapons and ammo from Joe's truck into the corner. The pile grew fast, and by the time we wrapped up, the scent of something delicious drifted on the breeze.

"Dinner's calling," I said. "Let's head back. I'll grab something first, meet you at the bunkhouse."

I detoured to the house to stop at the liquor cabinet on the way to the bunkhouse and pulled out a bottle of fifteen-year-old scotch. A quiet nod to the day we'd just survived, and the family we were building.

When I stepped into the bunkhouse, John spotted the bottle immediately.

"What's the occasion?"

"We made it," I said simply. "New friends. New family."

He nodded. "That's worth raising a glass."

"You boys like scotch?"

"Does it have alcohol?" Nick deadpanned.

"Dumb question for this crowd."

I grabbed some red Solo cups and poured a generous round, starting with Chef C, who took his with a theatrical sniff and nod. The others followed suit.

"Let it breathe a minute," I said, swirling mine. "You'll get a smoky nose, caramel mid, and a bit of vanilla on the finish."

Matthew raised his cup. "Fancy words for something that's going to burn real good."

Mel sat beside me, her presence a steady anchor.

"Hey, my sexy sailor."

"Yes, my love?"

"It's been a good day. We've got a real team here. I can feel it."

I nodded. "We do. We've got to start assigning roles, but we'll get there." I began mentally reviewing the plan. John over security, supported by the Marines and deputies. Chef C is running the kitchen. Mel would manage the gardens and greenhouse, already brewing something secret in the back plot. Gail, Claire, and Tracy would set up the clinic. The kids—our future—would train alongside us. Bonnie and Isabella had enough experience that I could probably ask them to help teach weapons handling to the younger kids. I'd take on ham radio training and communication.

Before the event, I'd followed a prepper out of Mississippi named Kyle. He'd hosted weekly ham radio chats. I hoped—just maybe—he was still out there.

Chef C stepped away from the group to check on dinner and then shouted out the door. "Dinner's ready—roast beef, red potatoes, and fresh salad from Mel's garden."

Not that he needed to announce it. The savory aroma was practically dragging people to the buffet table. As per Mel's rule, the children served themselves first, while the rest of us waited.

Before we could eat, Isabella raised her hand. "Can I say grace?"

"Please do," I said, stepping aside.

She folded her hands and spoke clearly. "Thank you, God, for this food prepared by Chef C, and for uniting us with open hearts. May we find peace and prosperity here. Keep us safe under this roof built by TJ and Mel. Protect us in the days and years ahead. Amen."

Ruffus gave a small bark, tail thumping. His own canine version of "Amen."

Putting my silverware down on the plate, I stood and addressed the room. "I need a few hands to help bring the ham gear from the shop. It's time we find out what's happening beyond these hills."

John, Joe, Nick, and Gavin followed me. I handed the radio to John, the microphone to Joe, and the antenna and cable to Nick. Walking into the bunkhouse, I found a clear location on a shelf and connected everything. I opened a window and had John take the antenna and cable outside and set it up. The antenna had a stand that we could telescope up to help us transmit further. It took a few minutes to wire everything together and get it powered on.

I flipped the switch. Static hissed. I hit the button to scan the different frequencies, and then, just when I thought we might hear nothing, there it was.

A voice.

"Good evening, everyone. This is Kyle Johnson, speaking to you from a remote location in Mississippi on the Prepper Radio Network."

Everyone in the bunkhouse froze. It was like hearing a ghost speak.

"As most of you have figured out, the situation has deteriorated significantly … From my high-ranking military contact, I understand North Korea has detonated three EMP devices over the United States …" The room went utterly still. "… No power grid. No cell towers. No modern communication. But ham radio still works …"

Kyle's voice carried on, sharing what little he knew, promising to broadcast every Tuesday and Friday night. He mentioned nothing of the government's status. He offered no solutions. Just information, and a reminder:

"Please assist those you can and protect yourself and others if possible. Kyle, signing off. Goodnight, America."

The radio fell silent. No one spoke.

It was real now. It had been real before, but this … this made it echo. The world was gone. But we were still here.

And we weren't alone.

Excerpt from Book 2, Magic Revealed, Anarchy Reigns

Trouble at Joes

TJ

John and I sat on my porch, drinking coffee and enjoying the peaceful morning. He broke the silence. "What do you think is coming next?" he asked. "Since the attack, it's like the whole country's flipped upside down."

I sighed, eyes scanning the rolling hills of Freedom Ranch. That question hung in the air like smoke. The world outside had fallen into chaos—gangs fighting for control of the cities, neighbors turning on each other, and no word from the government since it all went dark. My gut told me the worst was still coming.

"From everything I've seen—what little intel we've been able to piece together—our country's collapse is accelerating. I'd estimate we'll lose seventy percent of the population before it levels out. Starvation, disease, violence … pick your poison."

John leaned forward, his brow furrowed. "We could see foreign troops on our soil. If we don't organize now, we might not have the strength to stop it."

"You're right," I said, scratching Ruffus on the head. He looked up at me with those soulful brown eyes, then—no lie—gave a little nod and grinned like he understood. He placed a paw on my leg and patted me gently. I glanced at John, hoping he'd seen it too.

"Did you just see ... never mind." I stood and stretched. "We need to continue preparing our people. We need to be ready to fight."

"How's the security team holding up?" I asked.

"They're sharp," John replied. "Young, skilled, and motivated. The Marines and deputies train hard. We could use more boots on the ground, but for now, we're holding the line."

"Good. We'll need more than warriors to survive this, though. Gardeners, seamstresses, mechanics. And we'll need to strengthen ties with the town. If the gangs lock it down, we're going to be cut off from too many resources. Another flu sweeping through without meds? That'd be a death sentence." I rubbed my temples. "Ugh. I need more coffee—and Tylenol. Too much scotch last night. Talking with Kyle about the EMP didn't help."

John chuckled. "You Navy guys never could drink us Army boys under the table. We just let you think you had."

I laughed. "Oh, it's on. You Army types went from eating crayons to chewing pencils."

Gavin stepped onto the porch just in time to catch the tail end. "Not funny, guys."

"Easy, Marine. You can graduate to pencils someday." I snickered. "But seriously—we're lucky to have you and your team."

He muttered something I didn't catch and walked off toward the bunkhouse. Probably a Marine thing. I let it slide.

"He'll be fine," I told John. "We're all adjusting."

"Maybe we should gather everyone, light a campfire, and sing Kumbaya," John joked.

"You laugh, but a night like that might be exactly what we need."

Heading inside, I kissed Mel awake, handing her some hot tea.

"Well, butter my rum! You're so sweet, Darlin'." She smiled, sipping it.

"No more sailor mouth?" I teased.

"I'm working on it," she harrumphed.

Even in the morning light, Mel was breathtaking. Her shoulder-length brown hair had that perfect bedhead chaos. Lavender eyes, flawless skin, and a confident spark that never dulled. But her beauty wasn't why I loved her. It was her heart, her grit, her mind. Organized, thoughtful, compassionate. She was the glue of our community.

"What are you staring at?" Mel laughed, poking me.

"The love of my life," I said.

She shoved me off the bed. "You're too much." She winked, sauntered toward the shower, hips swaying.

I followed, tearing off my shirt. "Yippee Ki Yay!"

Later, Ruffus was waiting on the porch, tail wagging. He barked once and took off toward the bunkhouse, hungry for Chef C's breakfast.

Hand in hand, Mel and I followed. Inside, laughter and chatter filled the air. People talked about anything but the chaos outside. I scanned the room—something was off.

"Where's Joe?" I asked. "He's never late. That man could smell bacon from a mile off."

Mel squeezed my hand. I felt her tense.

"It's okay, love. Don't worry."

"Madison and Quinn are on watch," Russell said. "Want them to check Joe's place?"

"Yeah. That old Marine might've finally kicked the bucket," I joked.

Mel shot me a look. I winced.

"That old Marine's going to outlive us all," Gavin muttered through a mouthful of bacon.

Russell keyed the radio. "Security team, have you seen Joe today?"

"Negative. No sign yet."

"Go check his house. Report back ASAP."

"Copy that."

Mel's grip tightened. "You think he's okay?"

"I don't know," I said, holding her. "But I'll bring him back to you. I promise."

She nodded against my chest. Joe was like a father to her.

Fifteen minutes later, Madison's voice crackled through the radio. "Grab your gear. We've got a situation."

"On our way. Full kit?" Matthew asked.

"Yes."

"Roger."

Mel shot to her feet, but I stepped in front of her.

"Please stay here. I'll radio once I know more. If we need backup, I'll call."

"Son of a Brisket!" she growled. "You're not my boss."

"Just work with me. I'll make it up to you."

She sat with Gail and Shelly, clutching her radio like a lifeline. "Don't forget," she called after me.

"I won't," I said, kissing her head before sprinting toward the armory. Ruffus bounded beside me, ears pinned and ready.

"Let's go, Ruffus. Joe's in trouble—and your mama needs that old man."

Characters

TJ (Theodore James) Bush - Retired Navy, professional shooter and trainer

Melanie (Mel) Bush - Prepper, blogger/creative hobbyist, horticulturist, amateur archeologist

Ruffus - TJ's trained service dog

Gail Adler - Veterinarian

Katie Adler (14)

John Packard - Retired Army special forces soldier, Tactical training instructor

Shelly Packard-Prepper blogger

Joe Brown - Retired Marine Gunnery Sergeant and neighbor

Clarence (Chef C) Claydesta - Chef

Annette (Ann)Claydesta

Brian Claydesta (15)

Bonnie Claydesta (17) -Security

Billy Primm - Security and Maintenance

Joanne Primm - Teacher

Charlie Primm (14)

Melissa Primm (15)

Tracy Cole - Trauma nurse

Claire Westland - Trauma nurse

Matthew (Matt) Clean - Deputy Sheriff

Jolene Clean - Secretary

Isabella Clean (17)-Security

Blake Clean (12)

Russell Toume - Deputy Sheriff

Scarlett Toume -Dental Hygienist

Henry Toume (16)

Noah Toume (14)

Dylan Hart - Deputy Sheriff

Cole Whitlock - Deputy Sheriff

Madison Quill - Deputy Sheriff

Quinn Pherson - Deputy Sheriff

Nick White - Marine from the VFW

Gavin Smith - Marine from the VFW

Carlos Tejas - Marine from the VFW

Kyle Johnson - Retired Navy Chief Petty Officer, prepper, gunsmith, and ham radio operator in Mississippi

I would love to hear from my readers. You can leave me feedback on where you got this book, send me a note to **todd.ockert.author@gmail.com**, or visit my website at **toddockert-author.com**. I will post the new storylines to the blog and update them accordingly.

Please leave reviews on Amazon and Goodreads. They help boost our books' rankings on both sites.

You can also find me on Facebook at Todd Ockert–Author.

About the Author

Todd Ockert lives in West Texas with his wife. After a twenty-six-year career in the U.S. Navy, he retired and worked for an oil and gas company for fifteen years. A passionate reader, Todd averages around one hundred books per year. He's especially drawn to post-apocalyptic stories—though he doesn't have a favorite author in the genre.